EATER OF THE PACK

Fargo spun.

The three remaining wolves had ringed the Ovaro. Snarling and snapping, they leaped at its legs and its belly.

Rearing, the stallion flailed with its heavy hooves and there was the sharp *crack* of splintering bones. The Ovaro kicked out with its back legs and sent another wolf tumbling.

The third wolf had crouched and waited for its chance. Now it saw it. With a powerful bound, it sprang at the Ovaro's unprotected throat. . . .

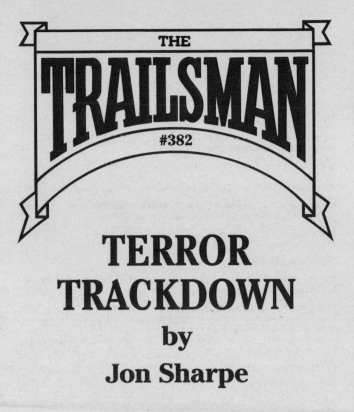

THE

TRAILSMAN

#382

TERROR
TRACKDOWN

by

Jon Sharpe

A SIGNET BOOK

SIGNET
Published by the Penguin Group
Penguin Group (USA) Inc., 375 Hudson Street,
New York, New York 10014, USA

USA | Canada | UK | Ireland | Australia | New Zealand | India | South Africa | China

Penguin Books Ltd., Registered Offices: 80 Strand, London WC2R 0RL, England
For more information about the Penguin Group visit penguin.com.

First published by Signet, an imprint of New American Library,
a division of Penguin Group (USA) Inc.

First Printing, August 2013

The first chapter of this book previously appeared in *Bowie's Knife*, the three
hundred eighty-first volume in this series.

Ⓖ REGISTERED TRADEMARK—MARCA REGISTRADA

ISBN 978-0-451-41759-6

Printed in the United States of America
10 9 8 7 6 5 4 3 2 1

ALWAYS LEARNING   **PEARSON**

The Trailsman

Beginnings . . . they bend the tree and they mark the man. Skye Fargo was born when he was eighteen. Terror was his midwife, vengeance his first cry. Killing spawned Skye Fargo, ruthless, cold-blooded murder. Out of the acrid smoke of gunpowder still hanging in the air, he rose, cried out a promise never forgotten.

The Trailsman they began to call him all across the West: searcher, scout, hunter, the man who could see where others only looked, his skills for hire but not his soul, the man who lived each day to the fullest, yet trailed each tomorrow. Skye Fargo, the Trailsman, the seeker who could take the wildness of a land and the wanting of a woman and make them his own.

1861, just over the Divide—someone makes the mistake of stealing a certain Ovaro.

1

The wolves came out of the timber at a run.

Skye Fargo wasn't expecting trouble. He had crossed the Divide over Berthoud Pass and was winding down Clear Creek Canyon toward the Fraser River. Lower down were the foothills and the distant city of Denver.

The only things on his mind were whiskey, cards and women, not necessarily in that order. A big man, wide at the shoulders and slim at the hips, he wore buckskins, boots and a high-crowned hat, along with a red bandanna and a Colt that had seen a lot of use. He was looking forward to a week without a care in the world. He planned to spend it indulging in what some would call wild shenanigans and others would brand downright sinful. He aimed to get lucky, get drunk and get laid, and again, not necessarily in that order.

The army's campaign against a band of Modocs had taken a lot out of him. The renegades proved hard to find, and once found, proved that they were serious about fighting the white man to the last warrior.

Now Fargo had time to himself, and he couldn't wait to taste the treats that gave his life spice.

When the three wolves broke out of pines about two hundred yards to the south, Fargo wasn't alarmed. Wolves hardly ever went after people. They didn't attack horses often, either.

At first sight he figured they were after deer or some other game. But then he saw that they weren't paralleling the tree line. They were coming straight toward him. They were coming fast, too.

Bodies low to the ground, ears back, their tails straight, they flew toward him and the Ovaro in a beeline that left no doubt as to their purpose.

"What the hell?" Fargo blurted. He thought about jerking his Henry rifle from the saddle scabbard, but why bother? The Ovaro had a big enough lead that it could outrun them. Jabbing his spurs, he brought the stallion to a gallop.

They were on a flat stretch but soon he came to a slope and had to slow. Glancing back, he saw that the wolves were still about a hundred and eighty yards away, give or take a few. He flew down the slope to another flat and used his spurs.

It wasn't half a minute later that he glanced back again and realized he had miscalculated. The wolves weren't directly behind him; they were closing at an angle. Already they'd cut the distance to a hundred and fifty yards and now they were coming on even faster.

"Damn." Fargo urged the Ovaro to its peak and realized something else.

The stallion was tired. They'd been on the go for a lot of days, from sunrise to sunset, pushing hard over some of the most rugged country on the continent.

Still, Fargo had unbounded confidence in his mount. It had saved his hash more times than he could count. Its stamina was exceptional. Even tired, it should be able to leave the wolves breathing its dust.

But when Fargo looked over his shoulder yet again, the wolves were another twenty to thirty yards nearer. They were big and in their prime and over short distances they could bring down a moose or an elk.

Or a horse.

His jaw muscles twitching in anger, Fargo rode as if the Ovaro's life depended on it. Which it did.

They'd been through too much together. Some folks might deem it silly but he regarded the stallion as more of a pard than an animal. It was a friend, and he'd be damned if he'd let anything happen to it.

Another slope loomed. This one was steeper and littered with boulders, forcing Fargo to slow even more. At the bottom he snapped his head around and genuine worry blossomed.

The wolves weren't more than a hundred yards away.

"Son of a bitch."

Fargo began to think about making a stand. Find a spot

he could defend and resort to the Henry. If he picked off the fastest wolf, the rest might scatter.

He'd tangled with wolves before. Most were spooked by the sound of gunfire.

That gave him an idea. Drawing his Colt, he shifted in the saddle. He doubted he'd hit them but he fired two swift shots anyway, hoping the blasts would bring them to a stop or cause them to veer away.

No such luck. The three lupine killers came on as determinedly as ever.

Fargo swore more colorfully. He'd gone from being angry to outright mad.

Here he was, minding his own business, and these jackass wolves had taken it into their heads that he and the Ovaro would make a fine feast.

He shoved the Colt into his holster and concentrated on riding.

The next time he glanced back the wolves were only seventy-five yards back.

Fargo needed to find a spot soon. He was at a narrow point in the valley, with forest to the north and the south. Trying to reach it would be pointless. Heavy timber would slow the Ovaro even more, and give the wolves the advantage of cover. He needed to fight them in the open.

Ahead was a flat area, maybe half an acre in extent. There were a few boulders but they were small and a few trees but they were far apart.

"There," he said to himself.

On reaching it, Fargo hauled on the reins so sharply, the Ovaro slid to a stop on its haunches. He was out of the saddle before it stopped moving, yanking on the Henry as he swung down. He worked the lever to feed a cartridge into the chamber, dropped to a knee and took deliberate aim at the foremost wolf.

By now the wolves were only forty yards away.

Fargo heard the Ovaro whinny and assumed it was because of the three wolves he was about to shoot. Then the stallion whinnied again and he risked a quick glance to find out why and his blood became ice in his veins.

Two more wolves were closing from the north.

It was a typical tactic. A pack split and converged on prey from two or more directions. And while the prey was focused on one group, the rest rushed in close enough for the kill.

Fargo was furious. He should have kept a lookout for more. He fixed a quick bead on the first wolf to the west and smoothly stroked the trigger. At the boom, the wolf went into a roll but was on its paws again in a twinkling and running strong.

Fargo worked the lever to fire again. Things had gone to hell and now it was do or die. He fired again and the first wolf's legs buckled and slid to a stop and this time it didn't rise.

Whirling, Fargo snapped a shot at the wolves to the north but he must have missed because the wolf he shot at didn't slow or stumble.

This was bad. Four wolves, two thirty yards to the west and two about the same to the north. Grim ravagers, out to bring the Ovaro down no matter what. Odds were he couldn't drop all four before the wolves were on them.

Fargo took a step back thinking that if he vaulted onto the stallion and rode like hell he still might be able to get away, but his left heel struck a rock he hadn't noticed and before he could catch himself, he fell. He landed on his back and twisted to rise.

The wolves were so close, he could see the gleam of bloodlust in their eyes.

Snapping the Henry to his shoulder, Fargo fired. The wolf he shot at yelped and broke stride but didn't go down. He worked the lever and fired again and now there were only three but three was more than enough, and the three had reached them.

Another whinny shattered the air as Fargo jacked the lever. He hadn't quite worked it all the way when a hairy form slammed into him with the impact of an avalanche. The next moment he was flat on the ground with a wolf straddling him, and the only thing keeping the wolf's slavering jaws from his throat was the Henry, which he had shoved against the wolf's throat.

The Ovaro whinnied louder than ever.

Fargo could only imagine what was happening. The

wolves would go for the stallion's legs, and if they broke one, or got a good hold, they'd bring it down and go for its neck or its belly.

Fear lent him the strength to heave the wolf off even as fangs tore his sleeve and raked his forearm. Rising onto a knee, he shoved the muzzle at its face and sent a slug crashing through its skull.

Fargo spun.

The three remaining wolves had ringed the Ovaro. Snarling and snapping, they leaped at its legs and its belly.

Rearing, the stallion flailed with its heavy hooves and there was the sharp *crack* of splintering bones. The Ovaro kicked out with its back legs and sent another wolf tumbling.

The third wolf had crouched and waited for its chance. Now it saw it. With a powerful bound, it sprang at the Ovaro's unprotected throat.

2

In pure reflex Fargo let go of the Henry and streaked his right hand to his Colt. He drew in less than the blink of an eye. He fanned the hammer, his hand lightning. His first shot impaled the wolf in midleap. His second cored it as it dropped. His third ripped into its skull below its eye and blew out most of its brains in an exit wound near its ear.

Shifting, Fargo went to shoot again but the last two had had enough. As silently as they'd attacked, they loped toward the woodland to the south, never once looking back.

Fargo shivered. It had been close. Too close. Reloading, he stood and stepped to the Ovaro. The stallion was quaking, too, and stamped a front hoof.

"I know," Fargo said. "I know." He twirled the Colt into his holster and ran his hand along the stallion's neck. "God, I'd hate to lose you," he admitted.

The woods swallowed the wolves.

Fargo stared at the bodies. Abrupt violence was the way of the wilds. He was used to it. But this had caught him off guard. It reminded him, as if he needed the reminder, that he must never, ever let down his guard. All it took was an instant's carelessness and a man breathed dirt instead of air.

Reclaiming the Henry, Fargo refilled the tubular magazine and shoved the rifle into the saddle scabbard. He gave the Ovaro several affectionate pats, climbed back on and resumed his journey.

The Rockies were in their late-spring splendor. Ranks of pines were broken by phalanxes of oaks and stands of aspens. Cottonwoods thrived along the waterways, which flowed with runoff from the snow-crowned heights. The grass was green, not brown as it would be in the heat of summer, and wildflowers enjoyed their brief time in the sun.

From the eagles and hawks that soared the high currents to the deer and the bear that hid in the thickets and the squirrels and chipmunks that scampered and chattered, the wild things in all their diversity were abundant.

Ordinarily, Fargo would drink it in as a lush drank booze. But he was eager to reach Denver. The scenery was the last thing on his mind.

It would take days to get there, though, and the Ovaro was about done in. So he rode slow and stopped early each evening to give the stallion plenty of rest.

About the middle of a warm afternoon he spied smoke and reckoned it was a campfire. But when he crested a low ridge, lo and behold, in the valley below stood a cabin and a small barn with a corral. The soil had been tilled and two small children were playing with a dog.

Fargo almost went around. He had no interest in settlers. They irritated him, there were so many of them. At the rate people were streaming to the West from east of the Mississippi River, in another hundred years or so the land west of the Mississippi would be as populated as the land east of it. He hated the mere notion.

Then Fargo thought of the Ovaro, and how the settler might have oats, and he gigged the stallion toward the cabin.

The dog spotted him and barked. The kids looked and ran inside. A minute later out came two women. Both had rifles.

Fargo expected a man to come out but none did. A friendly smile on his face, he approached at a walk with his hands where they could plainly see them. They didn't raise their rifles but they were suspicious and wary and ready to shoot. He drew rein and nodded at the kids peeking at him from the front door, then touched his hat brim. "Ladies," he said.

They were enough alike to be sisters. Both had flaxen hair and green eyes. Both had oval faces with high cheekbones. Their dresses were simple homespun, their shoes scuffed from work. One looked to be five or six years older than the other and had more pounds on her. She was the one who took a step and demanded, "What do you want here, mister?"

"I was hoping to put my horse up for the night," Fargo

said. "I'd pay for the privilege. Pay for grain, too, if you have any."

"We're not a hotel."

"Cassie," the younger woman said quietly.

"Hush, Carrie. He's a stranger."

Fargo grinned. "Cassie and Carrie?"

"Our ma was fond of C names," Carrie said. "Her own name was Constance."

"I told you to hush," Cassie said. To Fargo she said, "You can just mosey on."

"Where's the man of the place?" Fargo asked.

"He's not here but we expect him back anytime," Cassie said. "He'd say the same as me."

"Usually I oblige a lady but my horse is plumb done in." Fargo took his poke out, undid the tie string, dipped his fingers in and held up a double eagle. "You did hear me say I'm willing to pay."

"My God, sis," Carrie said, "that's twenty dollars."

Fargo knew that hardscrabble homesteaders like these barely scraped by. He was offering them more than they probably had to their name. "All I want is some feed for my horse. I'll bed down wherever you say and stay out of your hair."

Cassie hesitated. She clearly didn't want to but she couldn't take her eyes off the double eagle.

"Harold would say yes," Carrie said. "You know he would."

Cassie's mouth became a slit. "Yes," she reluctantly agreed. "I reckon he would." She trained her rifle on Fargo. "But first we find out who you are, mister. For all I know, you could be an owlhoot."

Fargo gave her his name. "I'm a scout."

"How about you hand over your six-gun and that long gun I see poking out of your saddle and maybe I'll consider it?"

"No," Fargo said.

"I'm not asking," Cassie said.

"Sis, no," Carrie broke in. "That's going too far. You can't leave a man defenseless."

"He doesn't need guns," Cassie insisted.

"What if the Utes pay us another visit? Or that Trayburn fella sends some of his men, like before?"

"Trayburn?" Fargo said. The handle rang the faintest of bells.

They ignored him and Cassie said to Carrie, "Quit carping. I have you and me and the sprouts to think of."

"I'm not out to harm anybody, ma'am," Fargo said. "Look at my horse, at how tuckered out he is. All I want is some feed."

Cassie looked at the stallion and then at the double eagle and licked her lips. "All right. I'll let you keep your hardware but no shenanigans."

"I won't cause a lick of trouble," Fargo assured her.

Yet as he said it, he couldn't help but admire the younger sister's shapely body and full lips.

"I hope to heaven you don't," Cassie said. "Do anything that makes me think you're up to no good and I'll put a bullet in your brainpan. So help me God."

3

Fargo tried to get Carrie's luscious body out of his head but it was impossible to do with her standing around watching him strip the Ovaro and place the stallion in the corral and carry his saddle and bedroll around to the side of the barn and spread his bedroll out.

Her legs were damned distracting, the way her dress clung to them as if it was painted on and left little to the imagination when she moved. From her thighs to her toes, she was right fine.

"Why do you keep looking at me that way?" she broke her silence.

"What way?" Fargo rejoined.

"Like when you look at me it hurts you."

"It does," Fargo said, placing his saddle where it would serve as his pillow.

"That's loco," Carrie said. "What about me can possibly cause you pain?"

Fargo grinned. "Hankering to see you without that dress on and not being able to."

Carrie snorted, and covered her mouth, and laughed. When she lowered her hand she said, "Listen to you. I bet you try that line with all the ladies."

"Just the ones I want to see naked."

"You did hear my sister mention no shenanigans or she'd splatter your brains?"

Before Fargo could answer, the cabin door opened and out came Cassie. She still had her rifle. "I saw you two jawing out the window. What are you talking about?"

"Nothing much," Carrie said.

Fargo inwardly smiled. If she'd minded his advances, she

would have told her sister. "I was asking about the wolves hereabouts," he lied. "Five of them tried to bring my horse down earlier. We barely got away with our hides."

"You don't say," Carrie said. "It must be the same pack that's been bothering us. They took all our chickens and a calf, besides."

Cassie nodded. "That's partly why my husband went off to Estes Park. He went to see about getting some laying hens and supplies."

"If only that's all he does," Carrie said.

Cassie shot her a sharp look.

Fargo had heard of Estes Park but never been there. It got its start only a couple of years ago when, if he recollected rightly, someone from Missouri decided a mile and a half above sea level was as high as they were willing to climb, and planted roots. "They have a general store there, I take it?" He wondered if they also had a saloon or two. It might do to stop on his way down to Denver.

Cassie nodded. "The whole family goes there every other month or so. It's a nice, peaceful community."

"Except for Trayburn," Carrie said.

There was that name again. "Where have I heard of him?" Fargo wondered out loud.

"In the Good Book," Carrie said. "His real name is Satan."

Cassie turned on her. "Enough of that. I won't have blasphemy around the children."

"They're inside," Carrie said.

"I don't care. They might hear you."

"I'm only speaking the truth," Carrie defended herself. "Ransom Trayburn is about the most evil man alive."

Suddenly Fargo remembered. There'd been a shooting affray in Denver not that long ago. A gent by the name of Kiley Strake, who worked for Trayburn, blew out the wicks of three hard cases in the middle of Larimer Street. It made the newspapers. "I seem to recollect he runs a lot of saloons and bordellos." He was going to say "whorehouses" but decided to be polite.

Cassie muttered something, then said, "My sister is right about one thing. Ransom Trayburn is evil. He feeds on men's weaknesses. That, and cheating honest folks. He tricks them into giving up their hard-earned money."

Fargo was curious. "Tricks them how?"

Cassie lowered her voice and said as if she was announcing a new plague, "He lures in those who like to gamble."

Fargo waited, and when that was all she had to say, he asked, "What's evil about that?" He liked to gamble, himself. Poker was a passion of his, up there with, say, naked women.

"He runs dens of iniquity," Cassie gravely intoned, "with their cards and their spinning wheels and their dice."

"Ah," Fargo said. Now he understood. He had met her kind before.

"I can tell by your tone you don't agree with me."

"No one forces folks to try their luck at games of chance," Fargo thought it worth mentioning. "They do it of their own free will."

"Ha!" Cassie said. "You call it free? When there are all those enticements? The liquor? The hussies? What man can resist all of that?"

Fargo had to admit she had a point. He sure as hell couldn't.

"Trayburn is a big gent in Denver," Cassie went on. "They say he has the politicians in his back pocket. That the law is under his thumb. That he does as he pleases and no one can stand in his way. That he has more money than he knows what to do with."

"That beats living hand to mouth," Fargo remarked.

"Are you trying to be funny?" Cassie said. "You haven't heard the worst part. He has men who work for him, gun hands and the like. All Trayburn has to do is snap his fingers and they'll blow out the wicks of whoever he tells them." She paused. "Or beat someone up."

"Beat them bad," Carrie took up the account, "so they can't hardly stand. Beat them so they are black-and-blue for a month of Sundays."

To Fargo it sounded like they were talking from experience. He was about to ask if that was the case when the dog barked and in the distance hooves drummed.

"That must be Harold," Cassie said, and smiled for the first time since Fargo met her. She started to turn.

Fargo doubted it. Not unless her husband had brought others. From the sound, there must be five or six riders.

He straightened, and sure enough, five men were coming down the valley at a trot.

"Oh, God," Cassie said.

"Speak of the devil," Carrie said.

"Who are they?" Fargo asked.

"Some of those gun hands I was telling you about," Cassie said, "and they are mean as can be."

4

Fargo had no cause to be concerned. He didn't know Ransom Trayburn from Adam. But he hooked his thumbs in his gun belt with his right hand close to his Colt.

The women moved so they were shoulder to shoulder, facing the newcomers. Cassie raised her rifle so it was level at her hip. Carrie clasped her hands so tight, her knuckles were white.

"You children!" Cassie hollered at the cabin. "You stay inside, you hear me? Don't you so much as poke your heads out or I'll blister your backsides so you can't sit for a week."

The dog stopped barking and showed that its backbone was mostly vocal cords. It whimpered and slunk around the barn as if in fear for its life.

The riders slowed. They bore the dust of miles on their hats and clothes. Two wore slickers such as cowhands favored but none of them bore the stamp of being cowboys.

Their faces were hard and cold and their eyes flinty. With one exception.

The lead rider was short, not much over five and a half feet. He had no shoulders and a wide waist, which lent him a pearlike shape. His face was pearlike, too. He had green eyes that seemed to be laughing at the world and a thin mouth that seemed frozen in an odd half smile or half smirk. He wore a small-brimmed brown hat, tilted back, and had a thatch of curly brown hair. His clothes were far better than those his companions wore. And the pearl-handled Remington he wore rigged for a cross-draw cost a lot more than a typical Colt.

When the short man drew rein, the others stopped. They leaned on their saddle horns and stared at the women.

Not the short man. He stared straight at Fargo and his laughing eyes narrowed. "What have we here?"

Cassie thought he was addressing her. "I told you before, Mr. Strake. You're not welcome at our place. Not now, not ever. Not after what you did."

Fargo's interest piqued. So this was Kiley Strake, the gun hand from the newspaper account.

Strake looked Fargo up and down and said, "Friend of yours, Mrs. Pulanski?"

"What?" Cassie glanced at Fargo. "Oh. Him. No. He's passing through and paid to bed his horse down for the night."

Kiley Strake glanced at the corral and his eyes narrowed as if he saw something that interested him.

Fargo looked over. All that was there were the Ovaro and two horses the Pulanskis owned.

"Did you hear me about not being welcome?" Cassie demanded.

Strake finally fixed his attention on her. The laughter in his eyes faded and was replaced by the same flint as the others. Only in his there was something else. Something deadlier.

Fargo had seen that kind of look before. It was the look of a natural-born killer.

"You don't seem to savvy, ma'am," Strake said. "What you want and don't want doesn't matter."

"How dare you?" Cassie spat.

"No, ma'am," Strake said. "How *dare* you and that husband of yours? You keep forgetting what he's done. He owes my boss money. And he's making my boss go to a lot of trouble to collect it. My boss doesn't like that. My boss doesn't like that one bit."

"Ransom Trayburn is an animal," Cassie said.

Strake sighed and shook his head and said to Fargo, "You try and you try to talk sense to some people and it's like talking to a wall."

"Don't you insult me," Cassie said.

"You want to talk insults?" Strake said. "How about the insult of your husband not making good on his debt? I thought

16

we made it clear the last time we were here that Mr. Rayburn doesn't abide insults."

"You made it clear, all right," Cassie said bitterly. "You beat my poor Harold until he could hardly stand."

"He was still breathing," Strake said. He gazed around. "Where is that no-account, anyhow?"

"He's not here," Cassie said. "He went off to Estes Park."

"We know that," Strake said. "We saw him there. And when I went to cross the street to talk to him, he spotted me and lit out like his backside was on fire. I told Mr. Trayburn and he sent us after him."

"Good for my husband that he got away."

"No, lady," Strake said flatly. "Bad for him and bad for you. Mr. Trayburn is at the end of his patience. Either your husband makes good or we take the money out of his hide." Strake smiled an icy smile. "And his hide ain't worth all that much."

Carrie coughed and finally spoke. "Are you saying you'd kill him over a little thing like money?"

"The amount's not so little, sweet cheeks," Strake replied. "And if Mr. Trayburn decides he wants your precious Harold dead, well . . ." Strake shrugged.

"I want you off our property," Cassie said.

Strake looked at the cabin and at the tilled rows and said, "I'll ask you again. Where is he?"

"I just told you he's not here."

"Why don't I believe you? We chased after him but lost his trail some miles back. He was headed this way, though. Now tell me where he is or this will get ugly."

Cassie stiffened her spine in defiance. "I've told you the truth, damn you."

Strake looped his reins around his saddle horn and made as if to climb down, then stopped and looked at Fargo.

"How about if I ask you, mister, instead? Is her husband here or not?"

"I haven't seen hide nor hair of him since I got here," Fargo said.

Strake nodded and unwrapped his reins. "I'm obliged."

Cassie gestured. "You'll believe him and not me?"

"He's got no reason to lie to me," Strake said. "You do."

"Yes, I'd lie to save my Harold," Cassie admitted. "I'd do anything to help him."

"Then listen good." Strake placed his hand on his Remington. "This is your last warning. Either your husband pays up or you become a widow. Do you hear me, bitch?"

Cassie started to jerk her rifle up.

Just like that, the Remington was out and pointed at her. It was one of the slickest draws Fargo ever saw. Cassie froze at the click of the hammer and her face drained of blood.

"Drop it," Strake said.

She let go of the Spencer.

Strake's hand flicked and the Remington was back in its holster. "You came that close," he said, and held his forefinger and thumb a hair's-width apart. "Mr. Trayburn isn't paying me to do you but I by God will if you ever try that again."

"You could kill a woman?" Carrie asked, horrified.

"Could and have," Strake said. He raised his reins, gave the corral another of those odd looks, and without another word, reined around and led his two-legged wolves off up the valley.

"Good riddance," Carrie said.

Cassie stooped and picked up her rifle. "You see?" she said to Fargo. "Sidewinders, every last one of them."

"I wouldn't want them mad at me," Fargo said. Not that he would run from them if they were. He could do without the nuisance.

"I noticed you just stood there and didn't do a thing," Carrie criticized.

"It's not my fight," Fargo said. "I'm not the one who lost money I didn't have."

"You blame my Harold for this?" Cassie angrily spat.

"Stupid is as stupid does," Fargo said.

5

The women went off in a huff. Fargo didn't expect to see them again before night fell but he was mistaken.

The last blaze of color dappled the western sky and twilight was about to descend when Carrie came out carrying a wooden tray with food.

Fargo liked how her dress swayed when she walked. He was seated with his back to his saddle, cleaning the Henry.

"This is a surprise."

"For twenty dollars you should at least have a meal."

Carrie hunkered so close to him, their arms brushed. "Cassie didn't agree but I brought you some food anyhow."

"Kind of you," Fargo said, setting the Henry and the ramrod aside.

"I'm sorry about how we treated you." Carrie placed the tray in his lap. As she pulled her hands back, she ran them across his thighs.

"Well, now," Fargo said. The aroma made his stomach rumble. A plate was heaped high with venison covered in gravy, with potatoes smeared in butter. Two thick slices of bread were to the side. Best of all, a large cup brimmed with steaming coffee.

"It's not fancy but it's filling."

"It's right fine," Fargo said. He picked up a fork and knife, cut a piece of venison, and bit. The taste made his mouth water.

"Mind if I join you?" Carrie said, sitting back against the barn wall.

"I'd have to be loco to mind the company of a pretty gal like you."

"There you go again," Carrie said, but she smiled.

"So when can you sneak out?" Fargo asked.

"I beg your pardon?"

"After your sister and the kids fall asleep. We can go in the barn if you're worried they might wake up and see us."

"We've only just met and you expect me to throw myself at you?"

"If it will make you feel better about it," Fargo said, "I'll throw myself at you."

"You don't fool me. I suppose if we did it, I'd never see you again."

"Probably not," Fargo said.

"At least you're honest." Carrie gazed off at the high peaks to the south. "That there is something."

Fargo was more interested in the food than in her rambling. He used the spoon to shovel potatoes into his mouth.

"A lot of men aren't so honest. Some pretend to be one thing when secretly they're another."

Fargo was in heaven. Hot potatoes and butter were as delicious as food got.

"They talk to you normal but in their heads something else is going on. They smile at you normal but behind their eyes is you, undressed."

Fargo swallowed and looked at her. She was still gazing at the far-off peaks.

"Honest men like you are as rare as hen's teeth. So I appreciate you. I truly do."

"I appreciate your body," Fargo said to lighten her mood.

She reluctantly tore her eyes from the glistening snowy summits, and smiled. "What a nice thing to say."

Fargo grunted and forked another piece of venison. It had been lightly salted and he chewed with relish.

"A lot of men aren't so nice. They put on a good show when they're around others. But when they get you alone for the first time they shove their hands up your dress and shock you half to death."

Fargo stopped chewing.

"I could never be a man and do what they do. It's obscene. A woman should have her decency if she wants it, shouldn't she?"

"I don't force women," Fargo said.

"No, I can see that. You treat us as equals. Would to God that all men were the same. Even the ones closest to you, the ones you naturally trust the most, can be wolves in kin clothing."

"Hell," Fargo said.

"I couldn't tell her. I just couldn't. It would break her heart and she's my sister." Carrie paused. "I don't know why I'm telling you. I've never opened up to anyone about it. And you're a stranger."

"Want me to pistol-whip him for you?"

Carrie threw back her head and laughed. A good, long, clean laugh that ended with a giggle and a grin. "You would, wouldn't you? Damn, you are something."

"You cuss a lot. You know that?"

She laughed some more and reached over and gently placed her hand on his leg. "You've done it, you devil. Why did you have to be so nice?"

"I thought Ransom Trayburn was the devil?"

"He's one kind and my in-law is another but you're the best kind there is."

"Make sense often?"

Carrie's face had softened and her eyes were practically adoring. "I'd never have guessed. Not with the package you come in."

"Package?"

"The buckskins and the pistol and the air you have of being as hard as a rock."

"I can get hard," Fargo said, "right quick."

"I bet you can." Carrie stood and smoothed her dress. "Cross your fingers and you might get to prove it, say about midnight." She turned to go and looked over her shoulder. "Take your time with the vittles. I'll be back in half an hour or so to collect the tray."

"I'll take my time with something else tonight," Fargo promised.

Carrie blew him a kiss and sashayed toward the cabin, her dress swishing.

"Looks like I'll be having dessert later," Fargo said, and smacked his lips.

6

She was true to her word. It wasn't much past midnight when a shadow crept from the cabin and flitted toward the barn. She had on a bulky robe against the chill of the high-altitude night. That was about all Fargo could tell in the dark. That, and she smelled of perfume freshly dabbed.

"Howdy, ma'am," he teased. "Nice night if it don't rain."

Carrie smiled and settled beside him on the blanket. Her face seemed to shine in the starlight. Her eyes were pools of need. "Howdy yourself."

Fargo touched her hair and ran his hand from the crown of her head to her neck. "Anyone ever tell you how pretty you are?"

"You don't need that," Carrie said. "The sugarcoating. I'm here. That's enough."

"Practical," Fargo said.

"Randy," Carrie said.

"I thought only men get that way."

"Women do too, but ladies won't admit to it because then they wouldn't be ladies."

"Female logic," Fargo said, "is no logic at all."

"Now, now." Carrie grinned and leaned in and pecked him on the cheek. "It occurred to me. I never told you my last name. It's Treach. Caroline Treach. But everyone calls me Carrie."

"It's good to know who you're making love to."

She slid nearer so her shoulder was against his. "You're lucky I was able to come. I thought my sister would never get to sleep. She's worried plumb sick about Harold. He should have been home by now."

"Strake and his men?"

"That's her fear, yes. I feel sorry for her. When she married him she had no idea he was how he is. She didn't know he likes to gamble so much. She can't get him to stop no matter what she does."

Fargo had run across more than a few to whom gambling was an addiction, the same as those who glued their mouths to whiskey bottles from dawn until they passed out, or those who visited opium dens day in and day out.

"She frets they'll lose everything on account of his being so stupid," Carrie said. "She's at her wit's end."

"Enough about him and her," Fargo said. He wasn't being unkind. There was simply nothing he could do. Harold Pulanski was a grown man and grown men made their own beds, as it were.

"Sorry. It's just on my mind an awful lot of late."

"Let's see if we can get you thinking about something else." Fargo kissed her on the lips. She was tentative at first, her mouth closed, her body slightly rigid. But when he kneaded her shoulders and slowly slid his hands lower to cup her breasts, she let out a little sigh and her lips parted to admit his tongue.

They went on kissing, with him fondling her, a good long while. She leaned on one hand and had the other on his shoulder.

When Fargo parted the upper part of her robe, Carrie shivered. He slipped a hand under and the fullness of her tit filled his palm. He squeezed, and pulled on the nipple, and she moaned.

Easing her onto his blanket, Fargo stretched out. He took off his hat and kissed her and lathered her neck. She was sensitive there, and squirmed and cooed. The more attention he gave her breasts, the warmer she became.

Undoing the robe's belt, Fargo spread the robe wide, baring her charms. From her inviting lips to her flat tummy to the silken smoothness of her thighs, she was a treat waiting to be tasted.

"What are you looking at?"

"You really are gorgeous."

"Stop that. There's no need, I told you."

"Most ladies would be grateful for the compliment."

"Practical, remember?"

That was fine by Fargo. It was rare for a woman not to lap up the little niceties. A gal who wanted to get to it, and nothing else, was a novelty.

Before he got to it, he removed his gun belt, shed his shirt, and loosened his pants.

"God, you have a lot of muscles," Carrie said huskily as she sculpted his abdomen with her fingers. She kissed his chest and ran her fingers through his hair.

Fargo explored every square inch of her. He caressed, he stroked. Time crept on pants of passion, and at last both of them were as ready as they would ever be. He spread her legs and slid onto his knees between them and aligned his pole.

She surprised him by reaching down and taking hold.

Her eyes widened and she gasped, "Goodness gracious. You'll split me in half."

"Haven't split a woman yet," Fargo said, and slid up into her. She was wet, and hot, her sheath velvet lava.

Fargo held himself still as her nails dug into his buttocks and her teeth nipped at his shoulder.

Her eyelids hooded, Carrie moved her hips, grinding in wanton need. "Do me," she whispered. "Do me hard."

Fargo obliged. His hands propped on either side of her, he rammed into her again and again. Each thrust brought a gasp or a groan or the flutter of her eyes in the transport of bliss.

As he hoped she would, she crested first. She threw back her head and arched her back and her legs were a vise around his hips. She humped, and spurted, and started to cry out and bit her lip to stifle the outcry.

Eventually she subsided and lay limp from her release. "That was something," she said in contentment.

"We're not done yet."

Carrie gave a mild start, and looked down. "Oh my," she said. "Oh my, oh my, oh my."

Fargo went on pumping. She gushed once more and then he was there, swept into the tide of currents as old as time.

Drained, Fargo lay on his side, facing her. He was about

to ask if she needed to get back when she asked him something, instead.

"Do you hear that?"

Fargo raised his head.

It was the slow clomp of hooves. A rider was approaching at an hour no rider should.

7

Fargo dressed quickly. He pulled up his pants and strapped on his gun belt and only then donned his shirt and hat. He was on his feet before Carrie, who lay listening to the hoof falls. "You want to be seen bare-assed?"

"Oh!" she exclaimed, and sat up and belted the robe. As she stood she smoothed her hair and asked, "Who can it be?"

How the hell should I know? Fargo almost answered, but didn't.

The rider was coming from the north, which raised his wariness. To the east was the trail to Estes Park and other settlements and eventually Denver. To the west was the trail to the Great Salt Lake and eventually to Oregon Country or California. To the north was nothing but wilderness for hundreds of miles.

A silhouette drew rein and the horse nickered.

"Who can it be?" Carrie whispered.

"Hush." Fargo was poised to draw. It could well be a hostile scouting the farm. Or an outlaw looking for easy pickings.

The rider came on again, slowly. He was making for the front of the barn and would pass close to them. He appeared to be looking toward the cabin and hadn't noticed them yet.

The horse did. It looked right at them but didn't whinny, not even when Fargo stepped in front of it and drew his Colt and pointed it at the rider.

"Hold it right there."

The man drew rein and bleated, "What the hell?" His hands were on the reins.

"Who are you and what are you doing here this time of night?" Fargo demanded.

"I could ask you the same damn question," the rider snapped. The man was tall, that much Fargo could tell, almost as tall as he was, but there was a lot less of him. He was a pole with clothes.

"I won't ask twice," Fargo said.

"Who do you think you—?" the man began, and stopped.

Carrie had moved to Fargo's side. "Harold?" she said. "Is that you?"

"Who the hell else would it be but a man returning to his hearth and home?" Harold Pulanski growled. "What the hell is going on here? Who is this fella? And . . . my God . . . what are you doing out here with him this late?"

Fargo remembered what Carrie had told him about her brother-in-law and an icy cold rippled through him. "None of your goddamned business. Get off your horse and keep your hands where I can see them."

Harold Pulanski might be addicted to gambling, and worse, but he didn't have a yellow streak. "Like hell I will. No one talks to me like that on my own place. No one."

Fargo was around the horse before the homesteader could guess his intent. Seizing hold of Harold's arm, he wrenched him from the saddle.

"Skye, no!" Carrie cried.

Harold hit the ground hard. He grunted and swore and pushed to his knees. "I'll by God wallop you."

Fargo pressed the Colt's muzzle to Pulanski's brow. "Want to bet?"

Harold froze. All of him except for his mouth. "On my own property, you do this. Who in hell do you think you are?"

Carrie said, "Cassie has been so worried, Harold. Men were here looking for you. That awful Strake who works for Ransom Trayburn."

"I know who Strake works for," Harold spat. "Why do you think I circled around? To be sure it was safe to ride in. They spotted me in Estes Park and I had to fan the breeze. For days they've been after me but I shook them off my scent."

Fargo stepped back. "You calm now?"

"I will be once you stop pointing that smoke wagon at me."

Fargo twirled the Colt into his holster. "For all I knew you were one of them."

"That gives you cause to shove a gun in a man's face?" Harold rose and adjusted his hat. "Who the hell are you, anyhow?"

"He's on his way to Denver," Carrie said, "and staying the night."

"Who gave him permission? You? Or that stupid wife of mine?"

"He paid her twenty dollars," Carrie said.

"Twenty?"

In that one word Fargo heard the raw greed of someone to whom money was everything.

"Well, that's different, I suppose," Harold said.

"It's a fair amount."

"More than fair," Fargo said.

"If you're done shoving guns at me, I have a horse to unsaddle and a wife to talk to." Harold took the reins and walked around Fargo saying, "Carrie, you shouldn't be out here. It's unseemly. Get inside."

"I'll do as I please," Carrie said. "You're not my husband."

"You live with us."

"That doesn't give you a claim. And I won't be living with you for much longer."

Harold stopped. "Where would you go? You don't have more than a few dollars saved."

"I know my own situation," Carrie said. "If I had my druthers I'd be anywhere but here, sis or no sis."

Harold opened his mouth to say something.

"You heard her," Fargo said.

"I don't think I like you, mister," Harold told him, and tramped off.

"Do you see how he is?" Carrie asked. "Do you see what my sister has had to put up with?"

"She married him," Fargo said.

Carrie didn't appear to hear him. Almost to herself, she said, "What I've had to put up with?"

Fargo turned to sit back down but Carrie gripped his arm so tight, her fingernails dug into him.

"Take me with you."

"What?"

"When you leave in the morning. Take me as far as Estes Park and I'll make it on my own from there."

"I ride alone."

"*Please*. I'm begging you. I feel sorry for Cassie but like you just said, she's brought it on herself. And I can't take any more of *him*. The next time he touches me, I'll kill him. I swear I will. And I don't want that. Please, Skye. In return for what we did."

"Hell," Fargo said. That was the trouble with giving a woman a poke. She always felt it gave her the right to ask favors.

"You owe me that much."

Fargo sighed. "You had this at the back of your mind the whole time."

"Sort of. I admit that. But I didn't make my mind up until just now when he showed up." She clasped his hand. "I'll ask you again. Please. Get me out of here before I do something I'll regret."

"Damn me and my pecker," Fargo said.

8

Fargo wanted to leave at first light but it wasn't to be. Carrie wanted to have a last breakfast with her sister and their family. She asked him to be patient, and hinted that if he let her have these last moments, she'd reward him later.

Fargo sat by the barn with the Ovaro saddled, plucking blades of grass.

It was pushing eight when Carrie emerged. She had a calico traveling bag. Cassie hugged her and she hugged the kids.

Harold stood apart, glowering. In the daylight he was no beauty. He had a sallow complexion and acne and wore a perpetual sneer.

Fargo stood and folded his arms. In a few minutes Carrie walked over, tears glistening. The family trailed after her, Harold farthest back.

"All set?" Fargo asked.

She sniffled and dabbed at her eyes and held out the travel bag. "Here you go."

Fargo stared at it. Surely not, he thought. "Where's your horse?"

"I don't have one."

"The hell you say."

"I figured we'd ride double."

"All the way to Estes Park?"

Harold Pulanski laughed.

"I didn't think you'd mind," Carrie said. "I won't slow you that much."

"It'll take days."

"If you don't want to take me, I'll understand. Don't feel obligated."

Harold laughed a second time.

Fargo fumed. It would tire the Ovaro more, carrying double. But to spite Pulanksi he said, "I gave my word." Taking the bag, he hooked the strap over the saddle horn. He mounted, shifted, and extended his arm. "Grab hold."

Carrie had to hug Cassie again, and then she had to hug the boy and hug the girl. Finally she gripped his forearm and he swung her on behind him. She wrapped an arm around his waist and said, "Ready when you are."

I was ready two goddamned hours ago, Fargo almost said. The feel of her breasts against his back held his tongue.

Cassie and the children smiled and saved. Not Harold. All he did was glare.

The cabin fell behind them and the dog yipped as if in parting.

"I'm so happy to be out of there," Carrie said, pressing her lips to the nape of his neck. "I can't thank you enough."

"You will tonight."

She chortled and rested her cheek between his shoulder blades. "I'm so tired. I hardly got any sleep."

"Take a nap if you want," Fargo suggested. That way, she'd be wide-awake after they stopped for the night.

"What if I fall off?"

"I'll leave you."

"Oh, you." Carrie playfully punched his shoulder, then hugged him. "This will be great fun."

That wasn't the word Fargo would use. The extra weight was harder on the Ovaro and having to look after her made it harder for him.

"Is it me or are you in a funk?"

Fargo wasn't yet but if she talked his ears off, he would be. He clucked to the Ovaro and was grateful when Carrie shut up. She surprised him by not saying anything the rest of the morning. It wasn't until midday, when he stopped in a grassy glade to let the Ovaro rest, that she stretched and smiled and turned into a chipmunk.

"I can't thank you enough for your help. It means everything to me."

Fargo grunted. He was pacing to stretch his legs.

"I mean it. I wanted out of there for a long time but I couldn't bring myself to leave my sister."

Placing a hand to the small of his back, Fargo arched his spine to relieve a kink.

"You could say something."

"You slept with me so I'd bring you."

"Why bring that up again?"

"What if I'd been a sweaty drummer with a wart on his nose? Would you have slept with him?"

"Depends on how bad he smelled," Carrie said, and grinned. "I don't care for stink."

Despite himself, Fargo chuckled. "A woman who uses her body to get what she wants. Who would have thought it?"

Carrie laughed. "Most females do. Even the married ones. Let a man have his way and he's clay in our hands."

"Brag much?"

"It's human nature," Carrie said. "Men want it, and women get to say whether they can or not." Her face clouded. "Unless the man is a pig like my brother-in-law. I should have stuck a knife in him. But Cassie would never forgive me and her kids would hate me for the rest of my born days."

"You could have pushed him off a cliff and claim he tripped."

Carrie giggled. "I like how you think. Believe it or not, I did consider pushing him out of the hayloft in the barn. But it might not have broken his neck, and if he lived, he'd be awful mad."

"And here I'd reckoned you were an innocent young thing," Fargo said drily.

"Cassie and me were orphaned young. We had to learn to survive on our own. One of our first lessons was that we use what we have to get what we want." Carrie frowned. "Why she picked Harold I will never know. I could have told her right off he wasn't good for her but the heart wants what the heart wants." She sighed. "If there's anything in life more fickle than love, I've yet to make its acquaintance."

Fargo smiled and went to stretch again, and stiffened.

A feeling had come over him, a familiar prickling of the

short hairs at the nape of his neck. They were being watched. He was sure of it. Slowly turning, his chin down so as not to give himself away, he scanned the forest out of the corners of his eyes. He saw no one.

The Ovaro nipped at the grass, showing no alarm whatsoever.

"Something the matter?" Carrie asked.

"Guess not," Fargo said.

But twice more that afternoon he felt the same sensation. Each time he stopped and scoured their back trail but nothing.

He did come on sign, though. Tracks left by five riders, heading east. Strake and the gun hands, Fargo reckoned. He wasn't worried about overtaking them. They were moving fast and were a good twenty-four hours ahead.

The big question: what was *behind* him?

He wondered if it might be hostiles. A roving war party would delight in stalking and slaying a lone white man and white woman.

But something told him it wasn't Indians. A vague feeling he couldn't account for.

By sunset they were miles lower than when they started. Firs and aspen had given way to mostly spruce and pines. Once they reached the foothills the vegetation would change again, with more oaks and some maples and other broadleafs.

Fargo chose a clearing beside a stream for their camp. Carrie collected firewood while he stripped the Ovaro. He kindled a small fire and put coffee on to boil and unwrapped a bundle of pemmican.

"What is this?" Carrie asked, giving her piece a suspicious sniff.

"Buffalo meat mixed with chokecherries and some bear fat thrown in. I got it from a Cheyenne gal. They don't usually mix buff and bear but she had the bear fat left over and figured, what the hell."

"I'm willing to try most anything once," Carrie said. She took a bite and chewed. "Not bad."

Fargo selected a piece for himself.

Just then the Ovaro raised its head, pricked its ears, and stared to the west.

At the same instant, Fargo felt the prickling on his neck.

It could mean only one thing. Whoever had been shadowing them had moved in closer.

9

Fargo stared at his tin cup so if anyone was watching him, they wouldn't suspect that he suspected. He said barely above a whisper, "We have company."

"Excuse me?" Carrie said.

"Keep your voice down." Fargo sipped and set his cup on the ground. "Someone is out there. I aim to find out who. I'll trick them into thinking I'm taking a piss and circle around. You're to stay put. If you hear shots or I give a holler, scoot to the woods and take cover."

"Hostiles, you reckon?"

"Could be anyone." Fargo touched the Henry, which was propped against his saddle, with the toe of his boot. "I'll leave this for you, just in case. You know how to use one?"

"I've shot rifles before. But what makes you so sure someone is out there? I haven't heard anything."

"Me either."

"Then what makes you think so?"

"When you've spent as much time in the wilds as I have, you just know."

"If you say so," Carrie said skeptically.

"Remember, hunt cover if you have to," Fargo advised. Rising, he turned and walked toward the benighted woodland, prying at his buckle as he went to give the impression he wanted. As soon as the darkness swallowed him, he palmed the Colt and crouched.

Carrie had folded her arms to her bosom and was staring into the flames as if things were perfectly normal.

Fargo waited just long enough for his eyes to adjust, then stalked deeper in. He circled, moving with the utmost caution. He was almost to the west side of the clearing when something moved. Freezing, he focused on the spot. It might be their stalker or it could just as well be a deer or some other animal.

The minutes crawled on claws of tension. Just when he was convinced that whoever or whatever it had been was no longer there, it moved again.

Fargo crept forward. He slid each foot slowly and applied his weight with care to keep twigs from snapping underfoot.

He still wasn't sure if it was a person or an animal—and then he heard a low cough.

Fargo flattened. It had to be a white man. No Indian would give himself away like that. Quietly parting a clump of grass, he crawled toward the skulker. He needed to be near enough that he couldn't miss if they swapped lead.

Fargo eased around a spruce that had limbs low to the ground and up and over a log. He didn't realize the log was rotten and it gave way under him with an audible crunch.

Fargo turned to stone but the harm had been done.

Someone bleated in surprise. Flame stabbed the night and thunder boomed and slugs cracked the air mere inches above his head. Rolling off, he fanned two swift shots at the muzzle flashes.

There was a crash but not of a body falling. It was the rending of undergrowth as the shooter bolted.

Fargo heaved up. Another muzzle flash made him veer. He tried to pour on speed but it was so dark and there were so many obstacles, he couldn't go all out.

From in front of him came the pant of heavy breaths and the stomp of retreating boots. A face glanced back, a pale blob with no detail.

"Stop!" Fargo cried, knowing full well he was wasting his breath. He veered just as the man's rifle cracked.

The slug hit a pine with a loud *thwack*.

Fargo fired but doubted he scored. He lost sight of the fleeing figure, and stopped. He thought that maybe the man had gone to ground.

A whinny proved him wrong.

He flew forward but he was too late. A horse and its rider were melting into the pitch of night. He raised the Colt but didn't shoot. He might hit the horse.

Fargo swore. He'd blown his best chance. From here on out their stalker would be doubly wary. Reloading, he listened to the hoofbeats fade. Giving chase would be pointless. The man had too much of a lead.

Disappointed, Fargo bent his boots to the fire. Carrie and the Henry had disappeared. Apparently she'd done as he'd told her.

Fargo strode from cover. "You can come out," he hollered. Squatting, he refilled his cup.

"My heart was in my throat," Carrie said as she stepped into the firelight. "All those shots."

Fargo grunted.

"If anything happens to you, I'll be all alone," she mentioned the obvious.

"Nice to know you care."

"Who do you reckon it is? What are they up to?"

"If I knew that," Fargo said, "I'd be a happy man."

He suggested she turn in and to his surprise she did without arguing.

He stayed up until past midnight, keeping watch. Wolves howled for a while but other than that the night was still.

Sinking onto his back with his head on his saddle, he tried to get to sleep. His mind was racing too fast. He needed to find out who was shadowing them.

Right before he slipped under, a way occurred to him.

He thought about it some more when he woke at first light. Risk was involved, but so was having an unknown at their backs the whole way.

Carrie listened to his idea, and nodded. "I'll do all I can to help. But what if they don't take the bait?"

"We'll be no worse off than we are now," Fargo replied.

Little did he know how wrong he was.

10

Fargo's plan was simple.

Carrie would ride on a short way and wait. He'd sneak up a tree, and sooner or later their shadow was bound to appear to pick up their trail.

Using the toothpick, he cut a short length of rope, then sent her on her way. He tied one end of the rope to the Henry's barrel below the front sight and the other end around the stock. Slinging the rifle across his back, he moved to a tall pine.

Halfway up was high enough, he reckoned. He could see for hundreds of yards in all directions.

The rising sun dispersed the last of the shadows. Birds warbled and an early-rising squirrel scampered about.

To their stalker, it would seem all was as it should be.

Fargo unslung the Henry and placed it across his lap.

If it turned out to be a warrior intending to count coup, he'd take the first clear shot he had.

Some might say it wasn't fair to shoot someone from ambush. Others might say anything was fair in love and war. While this wasn't war, it was a matter of staying alive. So fair be damned.

Fargo half expected their stalker to show as soon as the sun rose over the horizon. But no. The sun went on rising and the only living creature he spied besides the squirrel and the birds was a doe.

After an hour or so Fargo began to have doubts. After another thirty minutes he climbed down.

So much for his brainstorm. He wondered if he'd scared the man off the night before. If so, he'd wasted a lot of time for nothing.

Shouldering the Henry, Fargo hiked to catch up to Carrie.

She was supposed to have gone no more than a quarter of a mile and stopped to wait for him.

He enjoyed the walk. Butterflies flitted and bees buzzed. A jay followed him a bit, curious. A chipmunk that didn't like to have its territory invaded gave him a piece of its chipmunk mind.

The Ovaro's tracks were plain enough, and he made good time.

By Fargo's reckoning he'd gone slightly more than a quarter mile when a strange thing happened.

The tracks came to an end.

Bewildered, Fargo stared at the last set and then at the undisturbed ground beyond. "What the hell?"

It was impossible.

He walked another fifty yards, and nothing. Returning, he studied the ground closely. He was among pines, with a thick carpet of pine needles. He roved in a circle and couldn't find a single track. Widening his circle, he came to a boulder and drew up short.

A leg poked from behind it. A female leg, and it wasn't moving.

Fargo ran around. For a few seconds he thought Carrie was dead. Then she groaned. Hunkering, he quickly examined her. She hadn't been shot or stabbed but there was a knot on the back of her head the size of a hen's egg. Someone had snuck up behind her and walloped her good.

"Carrie?" Fargo smacked her cheek a few times and her eyelids fluttered. "Can you hear me?"

Her eyes opened and she looked about in dazed confusion. "Who? Where? Oh, Skye. It's you. What on earth happened?"

"I was hoping you could tell me."

"I don't know," Carrie said, and tried to swallow. "I came as far as you wanted. I remember climbing down. I tried to sit but I was too nervous so I got up and I was staring back the way I came when—" She stopped and weakly raised a hand to the back of her head. "Oh, God. Someone must have snuck up behind me and hit me."

Trying to control the fear that welled in him, Fargo asked, "Is this where you were struck?"

"I think so. Why?"

"Make sure."

"Are you suggesting they carried me? What on earth for?"

"Have a look around."

"If you need me to. But I don't know as I can stand on my own."

Fargo helped her and she leaned against him, her legs wobbly.

"Sorry," she said. "I feel downright puny."

"You were hit pretty hard."

"Who was it? Indians, you reckon?"

"They would have taken you, too," Fargo said, and that "too" knifed through him like a blade to the gut.

Carrie looked around. "Oh. Wait. This way," she said, pointing.

Barely curbing his impatience, Fargo let her bring him to where the tracks ended.

"This is where I was hit. I'm sure of it. Why did they move me?"

"To make it harder for us to find their tracks."

Carrie tried to straighten but she wasn't recovered enough yet. "I remember that blue spruce."

"You didn't hear anything? You didn't see anything?"

"No. I was looking back the way I came, and then there was a lot of pain, and the next I knew, you were holding me." Carrie stopped. "What's the matter? Why do you look as if someone punched you? I'm the one who was knocked out." She put a hand to her hen's egg and winced.

An icy fist closed on Fargo's chest. "It wasn't us they were after."

"What are you—?" Carrie stopped and looked around. "Wait. Where's your horse?"

"You tell me."

"They stole it? That was why they hit me on the head? All they wanted was your animal?"

One of Fargo's few fears had long been that one day something would happen to the Ovaro. Either it would be shot or break a leg—or be stolen. He'd had it taken before, but never for long. He'd always set out right away and managed to find it again.

But this time, as Carrie had mentioned, they were in the middle of nowhere. They were without a mount. Whoever stole the Ovaro could get clean away.

Carrie said the last thing she should. "You can always get another. It's just a horse."

11

Caroline Treach would never know how close she came to being slugged. Or that she tempered Fargo's anger by placing her hand on his shoulder and saying, "I'm sorry. That was heartless of me. I'd imagine that you care for it if you've had it a while."

"You have no idea, lady."

"We should search around for clues."

Fargo was already bending his knee. He'd noticed a few shallow depressions in the pine needles. "I'll be damned," he said, touching one.

"What?"

"Hides," Fargo said.

"How's that again?"

"It's an old Indian trick," Fargo explained. "You wrap a hide over a hoof so it won't leave much sign."

"Then it was redskins?"

Fargo hoped not. The Utes, the Blackfeet, the Crows, it could be any of them, and finding the Ovaro would be next to impossible. "Some whites know the trick."

"How will you tell?"

Fargo followed the depressions. It was soon obvious the horse thief was heading east.

"Toward civilization," Carrie said when he told her. "That means he's white."

Fargo grunted.

For the next several hours they hiked at a brisk pace. Twice Fargo stopped when he noticed Carrie was flagging but she gamely insisted they press on.

It surprised him that the thief wasn't making more of an

effort to hide his trail. Then they came to a stretch of rock hundreds of yards from end to end and almost as wide.

Fargo figured to cross to the east edge and pick up the trail again. But there was nothing. No depressions, no scrapes.

"He changed direction," Carrie guessed.

Fargo made a complete circuit looking for tracks leading away. He found none.

Carrie scratched her head. "Where could they have gotten to?"

Fargo was trying to reason it out. The horse thief had to leave the rock somewhere. The thief might have erased the sign by brushing the ground with a tree limb but he hadn't come across any brush marks.

"Do we keep searching or head on to Estes Park?" Carrie asked.

Fargo would just as soon hunt for the Ovaro from now until doomsday but he had to face facts. They had no water. They had no food. On foot it would take them a week to ten days to reach Estes.

He tried to recall if another settlement was nearer. It had been a spell since he was in this neck of the Rockies, and new ones might have sprung up.

"Whatever you decide is fine by me," Carrie said when he brought it up.

Her tone suggested different. It told him she hoped he'd head for Estes Park. He couldn't blame her. The wilds were doubly dangerous without mounts.

"Estes it is," Fargo said.

"Thank you. I'm terribly sorry about your animal. Once you get a new horse you can come back and look for it."

Which was exactly what Fargo intended to do.

They had gone a short way when Carrie said, "Oh my. It just occurred to me. Whoever took your stallion also got your saddlebags. They must have taken everything you own."

"Thanks for reminding me."

To say Fargo was mad was an understatement. He boiled with fury. It lent him energy as they covered mile after mile.

By about the fifth Carrie was huffing. She mentioned that her feet were sore and her legs hurt.

Fargo asked if she wanted to stop but she shook her head and plodded on.

All Fargo could think of was the Ovaro. Of how long he'd had it. Of the many times it had saved his bacon. Of all the country they'd crisscrossed in his constant wanderlust.

Whoever took it would pay. He wasn't one for making vows but he vowed then and there that he would find the Ovaro if it took the rest of his days and he would deal with the bastard permanent.

He wasn't one for boasting, either, but any son of a bitch who got in his way was worm food.

By sunset he'd fallen into a rare funk. He was depressed. If he'd had a bottle, he'd suck the red-eye down. Instead, he kindled a small fire for Carrie's sake where it couldn't be spotted by unfriendly eyes. Since his fire steel and flint were in his saddlebags and his saddlebags were on the Ovaro, he had to use two sticks. He was out of practice and it took forever to spark the kindling.

He'd just settled back to glumly stare into the crackling flames when Carrie pointed to the northeast.

"Look. There's another one."

A glow marked a campfire. Whoever made it had been careless.

"Let's go see who it is," Carrie said. "They could be white and offer to help us."

"They could be white and not want to," Fargo replied. "Or not white and not want to even more."

"We have to find out, don't we?"

The hell of it was, they did. Fargo was tempted to make her stay put until he made sure it was safe but the last time he'd left her alone, look at what happened. Reluctantly, he put out their little fire.

Carrie was already up and eager to go. "Maybe they'll have food they'll share."

"Or maybe not."

"Why must you be so cynical all the time? Can't you ever look at the bright side of things?"

"I just had my horse stolen," Fargo said. "Don't talk to me about bright sides."

"Are you going to pout about it forever?"

"You should shut up," Fargo said.

"What if I don't? Will you hit me?"

"Keep flapping your gums and find out."

Carrie stiffened and drew back. "I don't much care for how you're talking to me."

"Then don't talk."

"Why are you taking your horse out on me? What did I do?"

Fargo stayed silent. She was right. He was being pig-headed. It had been his idea for her to go on ahead while he waited for their stalker. Little did he imagine that he'd played right into the son of a bitch's hands.

They had to go almost half a mile.

Fargo didn't get his first good look at the fire builders until he was a hundred yards out. He'd taken it for granted they were white. Indians knew better than to make fires where everyone could see them. But this was a day when things that shouldn't happen, did.

First the Ovaro had been stolen.

And now the glow of the fire revealed that the ones who kindled it were Blackfeet warriors.

The Blackfeet, who were notorious for counting coup on whites as quick as anything.

12

It was rare to find Blackfeet this far south. Rare, too, that the four warriors were so young. Not one had seen much over twenty winters.

One of the four was admiring a fresh scalp. The other three were passing a bottle of whiskey back and forth. Near them lay a large pack, opened, the contents spilled about.

Five horses, not four, were tethered in a string.

Fargo put two and two together. Wanting to prove themselves, this young bunch had ventured into new territory. They must have come on a trapper or mountain man and now were enjoying their spoils. The firewater explained the fire. They were half drunk.

"Is that what I think it is?" Carrie asked in horror, her gaze riveted to the scalp.

"Hush, damn you."

"I'm commencing not to like you as much." She said it much too loudly.

Turning, Fargo clamped a hand to her mouth and put his mouth to her ear to whisper, "I won't tell you again. If they hear us I'll have to kill them and I don't want to kill them." He let go and she looked at him quizzically.

Fargo wasn't about to waste breath explaining. She wouldn't understand. Yes, they were hostiles. Yes, they'd killed a white man. But whites killed Indians all the time for no other reason than their skin was red and not white.

To those four youngsters, counting coup was how they earned manhood. It raised their standing among their people, much like white soldiers were promoted for brave deeds in battle.

Fargo didn't want to kill them. But he did want two of

their horses. "Stay close to me and don't make any noise if you can help it." He started to circle around.

Flush with excitement by their recent coup, the young Blackfeet were drinking and talking and smiling and laughing. Their elders would probably take them to task for coming so far south. But then, the young of all skin colors were always reckless and headstrong.

Fargo hoped they'd go on relaxing and not pay any attention to anything around them. He picked his way with care, avoiding brush that might crackle and limbs that might snap.

Carrie did well. She wasn't as stealthy as he was but the soft scrapes of her shoes and the rustling of her dress reached only his ears.

The horses were a dozen feet to the north of the fire. Only one had a saddle. Two were pintos, a favorite with most Indians, one was a sorrel, and another a bay. The horse with the saddle, the animal that belonged to the slain trapper or mountain man, was a fine roan.

Fargo kept one eye on the Blackfeet at all times. The warrior with the scalp was talking and the rest had fallen silent to listen.

An oak tree loomed. Fargo crept behind it and flattened, intending to cover the last ten yards on his belly. He took it for granted that Carrie would do the same.

He'd gone a third of the way when one of the warriors glanced in their direction. He doubted the warrior could see them. To be sure, he looked over his shoulder and bit off an oath.

Carrie hadn't gone to ground. She wasn't on her belly. She was in a crouch and looking at him and not at the warriors. She didn't realize that one of the Blackfeet was looking in her direction.

The Blackfoot appeared puzzled. Maybe he'd caught only a hint of movement or wasn't sure what she was.

Fargo slid his hand to his Colt. He kept hoping he wouldn't have to use it. He never killed unless it absolutely had to be done. Well, almost never.

The warrior turned to one of the others and said something.

Quickly, Fargo twisted, grabbed Carrie's wrist, and pulled her down beside him. He wasn't gentle about it, either.

She gave a sharp intake of breath and whispered, "That hurt."

Fargo didn't give a damn. The two warriors were looking toward them. The one who might have spotted Carrie half rose and peered intently at the spot where she'd been.

If they would just go back to their joking and laughing, Fargo thought.

The warrior with the scalp spoke to the one who had half risen and whatever he said caused all four to stare into the darkness.

Maybe they'll decide it was nothing, Fargo hoped.

The warrior with the scalp rose, and so did the others.

"Oh, no," Carrie whispered.

As slow as molasses, Fargo eased back the Colt's hammer so the click wouldn't be loud.

The Blackfeet were reaching for weapons. Bows for two, a lance for the third, and a tomahawk for the warrior with the scalp. He motioned with it and they spread out.

Fargo still held out hope. They might come only a short way. They might decide it was nothing. They might turn back. Might, might, might.

The warriors came to the horses and stopped except for the one who had glimpsed Carrie. He moved out of the circle of firelight, a lance gripped firmly in both hands.

Fargo aimed at his silhouette.

It was then that Carrie did the last thing she should do: she gasped in fear.

The warrior stopped. He'd heard her.

A new fury gripped Fargo. A fury at all the simpletons in the world. And fury at himself for letting her inveigle him into bringing her along.

A few heartbeats went by and then the warrior did as Fargo knew he would. He raised his lance, let out a war cry, and attacked.

13

Fargo heaved to his knees and fanned a shot from the hip. The slug cored the warrior's chest but barely slowed him. Howling in rage as much as pain, the Blackfoot let fly with his lance.

Throwing himself aside, Fargo fanned another shot. This time the slug caught the warrior in the forehead and snapped his head back as if it had been kicked by a mule.

The dead body took another half step and crumpled.

Carrie screamed.

The other three were closing. One had an arrow nocked and Fargo heard the twang of the bowstring. The shaft whizzed within a whisker's-width of his head. He fired and the Blackfoot toppled.

That left two warriors and Fargo had only two pills left in the wheel. Like most frontiersmen, he seldom loaded all six chambers. For safety's sake, the chamber under the hammer was left empty.

The other bowman was moving to the left for a clearer shot, while the warrior with the tomahawk had somehow disappeared.

Fargo aimed at the bowman. He squeezed at the same instant that the Blackfoot loosed his shaft. Fargo's lead smacked the warrior in the sternum; the arrow whipped Fargo's hat from his head. A fraction lower and it would have transfixed his skull.

The warrior went down and Fargo went to reload. A cry from Carrie warned him. The warrior with the tomahawk, the warrior who had counted coup on a white man and taken a scalp, had risen out of nowhere and was almost on him with the tomahawk raised to bash out his brains. Fargo flung his arm up and the tomahawk's long handle struck the Colt's barrel. The force of the blow nearly knocked him over. As it was, he fell onto his side and kicked out with his left leg. His boot cracked against the warrior's knee and the warrior's knee gave. The next moment the Blackfoot was on his good knee and swinging at Fargo's neck.

Fargo rolled, heard the thunk of the tomahawk striking the earth. Scrambling to his own knees, it was all he could do to stay alive.

The warrior came at him like a madman. Fargo twisted; he ducked. He avoided a blow that would have cleaved him from crown to jawbone.

Since he couldn't reload, Fargo resorted to a desperate tactic. He threw the Colt at the warrior's face and the Blackfoot jumped back. It bought Fargo the moments he needed to dive his hand into his boot and palm his Arkansas toothpick.

Again the tomahawk descended. Fargo met it with the steel blade of the toothpick. Metal rang on metal, and it was a wonder the knife wasn't torn from his grasp. He flung himself away to give himself space to move and the warrior came after him.

Fargo grabbed the tomahawk by the handle as it swept at his neck. He stabbed, and the warrior grabbed his wrist. Grappling, they strained this way and that. Neither could break free.

Suddenly dropping onto his back, Fargo drove both boots into the Blackfoot's gut. It sent the warrior stumbling.

Fargo rose to his feet as the warrior recovered his balance. They stared at each other, the Blackfoot glowering in hate, Fargo wishing it hadn't come to this.

He knew enough Blackfeet to say, "I do not want to hurt you."

"You die, white dog," the young warrior spat.

"Go," Fargo urged. "I will not try to stop you."

The warrior gestured at his fallen friends. "For them I will cut out your heart and lift your hair."

"You will try."

The warrior attacked in a rush. Older, more experienced

warriors would have come at Fargo slower and used the tomahawk's length to their advantage.

Fargo jerked away from a swing at his throat. He sidestepped a downstroke and avoided an upstroke and drove the Arkansas toothpick to the hilt into the warrior's chest below the heart. He rammed it up and in and swore he felt the heartstrings sever.

The young Blackfoot went rigid. His eyes widened and his mouth gaped and scarlet filled it. He looked at Fargo in disbelief.

"I told you to go," Fargo said, and twisted the toothpick.

The warrior cried out. His eyelids fluttered. In slow motion he deflated like a punctured water skin.

Fargo yanked the toothpick out and stepped back. "This is your doing, damn you," he said to Carrie without looking at her. "You should have gone to ground like I did."

She didn't respond.

"Did you hear me?"

Carrie gurgled.

Fargo spun, his anger evaporating like the morning dew. "No," he said.

She lay on her back, her mouth opening and closing. The feathered end of an arrow jutted from between her breasts, the feathers rising and falling with each labored breath.

Throwing himself down, Fargo gripped her hand. "Carrie," was all he could think of to say.

Her eyes seemed to focus. She struggled to speak and got out, "Sorry."

"No, it's me who should say that," Fargo said, and meant it. He'd treated her poorly, expecting her to be as stealthy as he was. And he was the one who'd sent her on ahead with the Ovaro. He should have known better.

She looked at the arrow. "Never reckoned," she gasped, "it would be like this."

"Hell," Fargo said.

"My own fault," Carrie said. "I was too scared to move."

Fargo growled deep in his throat.

"I wish . . ." Carrie began. But she would never get to finish, never get to say what the wish was. She broke into convulsions and she cried out, and died.

Fargo knelt there holding her hand a long while. Finally he let go and stood and looked at her and the dead warriors. The senselessness of it made him want to throw a fit.

Instead, he buried Carrie. He didn't have a shovel so he couldn't go deep. He topped the earthen mound with a log he rolled into place to keep the scavengers from digging up her remains.

He now had more horses than he knew what to do with. He went to the roan and found a few surprises. The first was a Sharps in the saddle scabbard. Why the Blackfeet hadn't taken it was a puzzlement, although some Indians did prefer their usual weapons over white firearms.

Fargo slid the Sharps out. He'd used one for years before he switched to the Henry. The only reason he did was because a Sharps was a single-shot while the Henry held fifteen in its tubular magazine and another in the chamber to make a total of sixteen. That much lead came in handy sometimes.

The Blackfeet hadn't opened the saddlebags, either.

It occurred to Fargo that maybe they'd counted coup not long before the sun went down, and flush with their triumph, they hadn't gotten around to examining their spoils.

He found ammunition. He found jerky. He found a letter written in a feminine hand to someone named Seth saying how much she wished he would pay their family a visit someday soon, and how much their ma missed him.

He also found a flask. He hefted it and shook it, and grinned.

Fargo opened it, wiped it on his sleeve, and sipped. Monongahela, by God.

For over an hour he sat at the fire, sipping and eating and nursing his temper. He didn't have much of an appetite so a few pieces sufficed.

All he could think of, yet again, was the Ovaro.

He wondered if there had been more Blackfeet, and one of them had taken the stallion. After all, the Blackfeet loved to steal a horse as much as they loved to kill a white. They loved it so much, they considered it the same as counting coup in battle.

Then again, it could be anyone. Horse thieves were as common as rabbits in some parts.

He'd long had a nagging fear that something like this

would happen one day. So far he'd been lucky but no one's luck held forever. The odds had caught up with him, and he hated it more than he'd ever hated anything.

Fargo turned in early. A good night's rest and he would be in the saddle at the crack of daybreak and after the horse thief. Whoever the son of a bitch was didn't know it yet, but they'd stolen the wrong animal. He would hunt them down if it took years, and when he caught up to them, there would be a reckoning—in blood.

14

To call Estes Park a settlement was being charitable. It wasn't any such thing. There was a saloon with an attached general store and some cabins and that was all. They were situated at the east end of the park that accounted for part of the name.

They had to be.

The "Estes" who accounted for the rest of the name was in fact the handle of one Joel Estes, who claimed most of the park as his cattle ranch. Gossip had it he—or his wife—was tired of the harsh winters and the family was fixing to head for warmer climes, in which case all that picturesque land would draw homesteaders like gold drew the greedy.

Someone was thinking ahead and had built the saloon and the store. That someone was Ransom Trayburn.

All this Fargo learned within ten minutes of striding to the bar and smacking down a coin for a drink. His first glass he tossed off in memory of the trapper; it was money from a poke he'd found in the saddlebags.

The bartender, a jovial soul with more belly than forehead, came back from refreshing another man's glass. "Anything else you'd like to know, friend?"

"I have some horses to sell," Fargo said. "Know anyone who might be interested?" He hadn't mentioned the Ovaro yet. He was leading up to that.

"Mr. Trayburn might be interested but he's not here. And they have to be uncommon good animals. Where did you get them?"

"From a Blackfoot war party."

The man's eyebrows crawled up his forehead half an inch. "You don't say. They're not the Nez Perce, who raise the best horseflesh anywhere, but sometimes they have good horses. How about I take a look?"

Fargo led him to the batwings and pointed at the four warhorses tied to a hitch rail next to the roan.

"They appear pretty average to me."

Fargo had to admit that as horses went, they were.

"I'm afraid my boss wouldn't want them. But there are always gents looking to buy one. I'll spread the word you're selling. How long do you aim to stick around?"

Fargo hadn't thought that far ahead. He needed to be shed of them and could use the extra money in his search for the Ovaro. "A couple of days at the most. Can I sell them in that time?"

"Tell you what. If we don't find a buyer, I might take them off your hands myself."

"Why so generous?" Fargo asked.

"Generous, nothing," the man said with a smile. "We get tame redskins who stop by now and then. Crows, mostly. Likely as not they'd love to get their hands on a Blackfoot warhorse, the Blackfoot being their enemies and all. They might be willing to trade for some prime furs I can sell in Denver for twice what I pay you."

"A gent after my own heart," Fargo said. He took his bottle and a glass to a corner table and sat with his back to the wall, as was his wont. He was on his third glass when perfume wreathed him and the chair across from him was pulled out by a buxom dove in a dress that had to be two sizes too small.

"Mind if I join you?" she asked, and sat before he could tell her he'd rather be alone.

Fargo sighed. Ordinarily, he liked that he drew women like honey drew bears.

"My name is Holly, by the way," she introduced herself. She had a lot of miles on her but she was well preserved. Hazel eyes sized him up as a butcher would size up a slab of meat. "My, oh my. Aren't you good-looking?"

"If you say so." Fargo filled his glass and shoved it across.

"What's the matter, honey? You sound down in the dumps." Holly raised the glass and said, "I thank you."

She downed every last drop in a single swallow.

"Damn, woman," Fargo said, impressed.

Holly pushed the glass back. "A refill, if you don't mind. And you didn't answer me."

"Someone stole my horse."

"Sorry to hear that, sugar," Holly said. "A lot of that goes on in these parts. What kind is it?"

"An Ovaro."

"That's a new one on me. What does it look like?"

"Like a pinto," Fargo said, "only the markings are different."

"I don't know as I've ever seen one," Holly said. "Or if I have I didn't know it." She brightened. "Say, there's a couple of pinto-looking animals out at the hitch rail right this minute."

"They're mine," Fargo said, "and they're real pintos."

"Oh." Holly drank only half the refill at a gulp, and set the glass down. "I can ask around."

"I'd be obliged."

Holly bent toward him and said huskily, "You wouldn't happen to be interested in more than a drink, would you?"

Yes was on the tip of Fargo's tongue. It came as naturally as breathing. But he surprised himself. Instead of yes, he said, "Not now, thanks."

"Is it my looks or what?" Holly asked, sounding slightly offended.

"It's me," Fargo answered, and said something he never thought he would hear himself say about *that*, "I'm not much in the mood."

"Well, if you change your mind, I'll be around." Holly winked and grinned and sashayed off to find a likelier prospect.

"Hell," Fargo said. His bottle in hand, he rose and went out. Leaning on a porch post, he drank in the scenery and the booze, both.

Estes Park was spectacular. It was called a "park" because in the old days that was what the early trappers called any high-country oasis with parklike settings. Here there was a lake and mile after mile of grassy meadows.

It was ideal for cattle except for one thing. The winters were hellacious. It got so cold, a lot of the cows froze to death.

Snow was visible year round. Not in the park itself but on the ring of high peaks that surrounded it. Some were nearly three miles high.

Fargo took it all in and didn't feel the admiration he normally would. He was in too deep a funk. That in itself was remarkable. He rarely let his emotions browbeat him like some folks did. He kept a tight rein except when he was mad.

Restless, he turned and went back in. He'd taken only a few steps when he happened to glance over at the poker tables and stopped cold in his tracks.

At one of the tables sat Harold Pulanski.

15

Harold was so intent on his cards and the other players that he didn't notice Fargo come up behind him.

A stack of chips was at Harold's elbow. From where Fargo stood, he counted pretty near five hundred dollars' worth. A lot of money for a man who less than a week ago claimed he was flat broke. An awful suspicion took root and festered.

"Are you going to bet or what, Harold?" another player asked.

"I swear," said someone else, "you're the slowest in creation."

"I need to think, don't I?" Harold protested. "Need to calculate the odds."

"Listen to you," the first man scoffed. "You can't calculate one plus one without help."

The others laughed.

"Go to hell, Jiggs," Harold said.

"I'm only stating a fact everyone here knows," Jiggs said. "It's why you're so piss-poor at cards."

"I am not."

"You lose more than all of us put together," Jiggs said. "It's what got you into trouble with Trayburn, we hear."

"I'm not in trouble now," Harold declared.

"Which is good for you," Jiggs said. "Those as get on his wrong side have a habit of not living long."

Another man snickered. "Ain't that the truth. The last gent alive I'd want mad at me is Ransom Trayburn."

"It's that Kiley Strake you have to worry about," mentioned the player who hadn't spoken yet. "He likes to kill, that one."

"Don't let him hear you say that," Jiggs cautioned. "And

63

Strake isn't the only gun hand Trayburn has working for him."

"Are we here to play cards or talk about killers?" a man groused. "I've raised the ante. Match me or raise me or fold, Harold, but by God, do something."

"I'm still thinking," Harold said.

"We can see the smoke coming out your ears," Jiggs said.

"Go to hell."

"I will admit," Jiggs said, not taking offense, "I didn't reckon on seeing you back here so soon. And not with that much money."

"What did you do?" another grinned. "Sell your wife?"

That provoked more laughter.

"You can go to hell, too," Harold said. He finally pushed out several chips. "I call."

"Jesus," the man who had raised said. "All that thinking and that's all you do?"

"You'd make a fine turtle, Harold," Jiggs said.

"I'll make a fine dandy when I strike it rich,," Harold said.

"Not that again," Jiggs said.

"We just had a gold rush, didn't we? Why do you think I dragged my family so far out? Cassie thinks it was to have a ranch. Hell, I hate ranching. But there are streams nearby I can pan."

"So you lied to your wife just like you lie to everyone else?" Jiggs said, and sighed. "Why am I not surprised?"

"What was that business about lying to myself?"

"We both know you'll never do any panning. You're lazy, Harold. The laziest son of a bitch I know. You'd rather work at cards if you can call the losing you do work."

"A man can dream," Harold said. He put his hand on his pile of chips. "And I'm not the no-account you brand me. Just yesterday I owed Ransom Trayburn over a thousand dollars. Now my slate is wiped clean and I have five hundred dollars, besides."

"How'd you work that miracle?" Jiggs asked.

Harold chuckled. "You know how much he likes good horseflesh."

"*You* sold *him* a horse?" Jiggs said. "Where in hell did

you get an animal Trayburn would be interested in? He only likes the best."

Fargo stepped around next to Pulanski's elbow. "I'd like to hear the answer to that myself."

Harold gave a violent start and nearly dropped his cards. "You!" he blurted. "How'd you get here so soon?"

"Why, Harold," Fargo said in simmering fury, "whatever do you mean?"

Harold gulped and set his cards down. "Nothing. I didn't mean nothing."

"Let me hear about the horse you sold," Fargo said.

"I found it. Bought it from an old trapper who didn't have no use for it anymore."

"Which is it, Harold?" Fargo said, his fury rising. "You found it? Or you bought it?"

Jiggs coughed and said, "What is this, mister? You're interrupting our game."

"My horse was stolen," was all the explanation Fargo was going to give.

Jiggs looked at Pulanski. "Harold, you didn't."

"I did nothing, I tell you," Harold said, and started to rise.

In an instant Fargo had his hand on Harold's shoulder and slammed him down into the chair so hard, the chair made a cracking sound but stayed upright.

"Here now!" Harold angrily cried. "You can't lay a hand on me like that."

"How long ago?" Fargo said.

"How long ago what?" Harold shammed ignorance.

"Did you sell my horse this morning? Yesterday? The day before? Did you sell him to Trayburn personally? Was he here at Estes Park? Or did you sell it to someone who works for him?"

Jiggs cut in with, "Trayburn was here until two days ago."

"Well, well, well," Fargo said, and smiled a smile that made Harold recoil. "This is about to get ugly."

16

Fargo had noticed at the homestead that Pulanski wasn't a coward. And now that he'd had half a minute to collect his wits, Harold came out of his chair swinging.

Fargo blocked a looping right and planted a left on Harold's chin. It rocked Harold onto his heels but he came on again, his fists chest high. Fargo ducked a straight arm to his face, drove his right into Harold's gut clear to his backbone, and followed through with an uppercut that sent Harold toppling onto his chair. Both Harold and the chair wound up on the floor.

"Damn," a man said. "I'm glad you're not riled at me."

Harold was on his back, half-out, weakly shaking his head to clear it.

Fargo stood over him. "I know the why. You sold my horse to Trayburn to make good on your gambling debt."

A gleam of alertness came into Harold's eyes. "I didn't, I tell you."

"I know the how," Fargo said. "You followed us after we left your cabin. Then circled around when you saw me send your sister-in-law off. What did you club her with? Your rifle or your pistol?"

"He hit Carrie?" Jiggs said.

"We know her," another player said. "She's sweet as anything."

"She's dead," Fargo said.

"What?" Jiggs and another man said at the same time.

"Because of you," Fargo said to Harold, "we were stranded afoot. Because of you, she died of a Blackfoot arrow."

Jiggs came out of his chair. "Son of a bitch. I liked that gal."

"Give him to us, mister."

"We'll beat the bastard for you."

"Who said anything about beating?" Fargo replied, not taking his eyes off Harold.

"I have a wife. I have kids."

"I have a horse," Fargo rejoined, "and you stole him."

Lunging, he grabbed the front of Harold's shirt and hauled him off the floor. Harold swore and lashed out but Fargo got a forearm up to block the blow and delivered three of his own, short, swift jabs to the mouth that pulped Harold's lips. There was a crunch, and blood and pieces of a tooth dribbled out.

Harold sagged, not quite conscious.

Fargo was aware that everyone in the saloon had stopped what they were doing and were watching. He didn't give a damn. He heard shouts outside and knew that someone was spreading word of the fight. He didn't give a damn. He held Harold Pulanski at arm's length and shook him, and the moment Harold stirred, he struck him just as hard as he could throw a punch.

Harold flew half a dozen feet and fell. His nose was flat and bleeding and his eyes were closed. His limbs quaked.

"Jesus," someone said.

Fargo strode over. He noticed a glass on a table with a finger's-width of whiskey, picked it up, and splashed the liquor into Harold's face. The man the glass belonged to didn't object.

Harold gasped and wheezed and opened his eyes. His pulped lips moved. "Enough," he said.

Bending, Fargo punched Harold in the gut. He punched Harold lower down. He picked Harold up and flung him and Harold fell onto an empty table. The crash was tremendous.

Slowly, his spurs jingling, Fargo stalked up to him. He slapped Harold's left cheek. He slapped the right cheek.

Again Harold recovered and uttered a snarl of frustration. "Enough!" he cried.

"Not ever," Fargo said. He gripped Harold's shirt and Harold hit his arm but it was a puny blow. Sweeping Harold upright, he drove his fist into Harold's belly. Once, twice, yet again. Harold folded and would have fallen but Fargo held him up, then shoved him.

Harold tottered against the bar. It was clear of drinkers.

The patrons were pressed to the sides of the room, near breathless, some in fear, some grinning.

Harold hooked an arm on the bar top to keep from falling. "Please," he got out. With his mangled mouth it sounded like "Plesh."

Fargo moved closer and planted himself. "Go for your six-shooter."

"Whash?"

"It's tucked under your belt," Fargo reminded him. "Draw it."

Harold looked down. He looked at Fargo. He looked at Fargo's holster, and Fargo's Colt. "No."

"Draw."

Harold rubbed his scarlet mouth on his sleeve and said, "No, I tell you. I'm no gun hand."

"I am," Fargo said, and the Colt was out and level as if by magic. He shot Harold Pulanski in the left thigh.

Harold screamed. He clutched his leg and managed to stay on his feet and bawled, "No! Please!"

"Jesus God Almighty," a man said. "I never saw anyone draw so fast."

"Where did Trayburn take my horse?" Fargo asked.

Harold was staring in horror at the blood squishing between his splayed fingers. "I don't know. Honest. All I did was sell it to him."

"Ah," Fargo said, and shot him in the right thigh.

Shrieking, Harold pitched onto his side. He cursed and thrashed and blubbered.

Fargo twirled the Colt into his holster. He shifted so he faced Harold square-on and lowered his hands to his side. He waited until Harold was spent and gasping for breath to say, "Carrie told me what you did to her. How you forced yourself on her when her sister wasn't around."

Harold whined.

"Go for your six-shooter or I'll shoot you in one foot and then the other and one knee and then the other and work my way up until you do."

A man by the window said, "God in heaven. We have to stop this."

"I ain't hankering to die," someone else bleated.

Harold had eyes only for Fargo. "Listen. I'm sorry. I'm truly sorry. You've hurt me enough."

"Would you rather it was a rope?" Fargo said.

"Oh, God," Harold said.

"That's what they do to horse thieves."

"Yes, but—" Harold stopped.

Fargo and every man there knew there was no "but." West of the Mississippi, stealing a horse brought a prompt lynching. There was no appeal to the law or the courts. You stole a horse, you were hanged.

"Your smoke wagon or hemp," Fargo said. "It's your choice."

Harold pushed against the bar and straightened. He slid his right hand near the butt of his revolver. Licking the ruin of his mouth, he spat blood. "I hate you, mister."

Fargo said nothing.

"A man tries to make good and you hold it against him."

Fargo didn't reply.

"It's not my fault Carrie is dead. How was I to know some Blackfeet were around? We haven't seen any in these parts in a coon's age."

Still Fargo didn't say a word.

"As for your goddamned horse, it wouldn't let me lead it off after I clubbed Carrie. So do you know what I did? I hit it between the eyes with my rifle stock. That showed it who was boss." Harold laughed much too loudly and his right hand edged toward his pistol.

Fargo was a statue.

"Cat got your tongue?" Harold mocked him. "That's right. I hit your precious horse. I made it bleed, you bastard."

Everyone in the saloon seemed to be holding their breath.

"Die!" Harold screeched, and he stabbed for his hardware.

Fargo shot him in the gut.

Screaming, Harold doubled over. He looked up and wailed, "Just do it, damn you! I don't deserve to be shot to pieces."

"Yes," Fargo said. "You do." He walked up and when Harold opened his mouth to cuss or scream, he shot him between his yellow teeth.

17

You could have heard a stickpin drop in the saloon.

Fargo reloaded. He stepped to the table where Harold had been playing poker and stacked Harold's chips. No one moved. No one spoke. Turning, he pointed at Jiggs, who had moved over by the wall with the rest. "Come here."

"Yes, sir."

Fargo pointed at the stacks. "These are to go to Cassie Pulanski."

"I know the lady. My wife and her are friends. We'll be sure she gets it." Jiggs paused and glanced at what was left of Harold. "She'll ask how her husband died. What do I tell her?"

"The truth."

"She'll hate you. She loved Harold. I never could understand why—he was so worthless."

"I'm obliged." Fargo had set his bottle on the floor when he walked up behind Harold earlier and amazingly it was still there and hadn't been knocked over. Snatching it up, he moved toward the batwings.

"Mister?" Jiggs said.

Fargo stopped.

"I savvy about your horse but you might want to let it be."

"Can't," Fargo said.

"That Trayburn has a lot of quick-trigger sorts working for him, and at least one of them, Kiley Strake, is as good as you."

"Met the gent."

"You have? Well, if it was me, I'd think twice. Especially with the rumors, and all."

"Rumors?"

"Hearsay," Jiggs said. "Trayburn buys an awful lot of horses. Only the best. Once he buys them, no one ever sees them again."

A chill rippled down Fargo's spine. "That's mighty strange."

"It sure is. No one hereabouts knows what he does with them."

Fargo placed his hand on his Colt and looked at the bartender.

"I don't know, either," the man quickly said. "And I'm not about to ask Mr. Trayburn. It's not healthy to pry into his affairs."

Jiggs said, "If it was my horse, I'd be worried. I'd be very worried."

"I'm obliged twice over," Fargo said. "What do you do for a living?"

"Me? I'm a farmer. I live down in the foothills and come up here once a month or so to play cards."

Fargo took out his poke, and a double eagle, and flipped it at Jiggs and Jiggs caught it.

"What's this for? You don't need to pay me to get the money to Cassie."

"The body," Fargo said.

"Oh."

Fargo started to turn, and stopped. He'd had a thought. "Come with me."

Jiggs nodded and followed.

Fargo strode out. There wasn't a soul in sight. The shooting had scattered them like chickens. He moved to the hitch rail and motioned at the four warhorses. "Sell these for what you can get. Keep twenty for yourself and give the rest to the widow."

"That's awful generous," Jiggs said.

"I killed her husband," Fargo said. "It's not hardly generous enough."

"You had cause."

Fargo moved around the hitch rail, unwrapped the roan's reins, and climbed on.

"Mind if I ask your name?"

Fargo stared.

"That's all right. Forget I asked."

Fargo gigged the roan and rode around to the side of the saloon and the well-marked trail to points below. He was almost to the rear when who should step out in front of him but Holly.

"Hold up," she said.

Fargo drew rein.

"I saw you in there. I saw what you did." Holly's face was lit with delight, as if seeing a man shot to ribbons excited her.

"Good for you."

"How would you like it if I do you? Here and now?"

Fargo was suddenly very weary of the world and most everyone in it.

"I have a room at the back, just inside. Climb on down."

Why not? Fargo thought. He hadn't slept much in days and it was a long ride to Denver. A little rest now and he could push on through the night.

Holly misconstrued his hesitation. "It's for free. I don't often do that but as handsome as you are, I really want to." She gestured. "And we can share your bottle."

Fargo looked at his left hand. He'd plumb forgotten he was still holding it.

A small tree served as a hitch rail. Unlike the Ovaro, Fargo couldn't be sure the roan wouldn't wander off. He shucked the Sharps and followed Holly in.

Ladies in her profession, the more experienced ones, preferred comfortable beds, for obvious reasons. Hers was almost as wide as a four-poster and the mattress was so soft, lying on it was like sinking into a pile of feathers.

Fargo had been with a lot of women in his travels but seldom had any treated him as Holly now did. She had him lie back and told him, "Leave it all to me."

She wasn't exaggerating. She did everything. All he had to do was lie there and enjoy.

Holly took off his hat, his boots. She tugged down his pants. She slid his shirt up his chest and kissed and licked his chest and his belly. She kissed lower.

She acted as if she was starved for it, which wasn't unusual, even for ladies who made their living as she did.

Once she had him ramrod hard, she rode him a good long spell, her back arched, her expression dreamy, her tits jiggling under his nose. When she exploded, he thought she'd break the bed.

He exploded, too, although he hardly felt it. It was peculiar. There was no pleasure, no tingles, nothing. He didn't tell her that.

"You were wonderful," Holly recited the line her kind used even when their lovers weren't.

Fargo grunted.

Afterward, they dozed.

Fargo wasn't much for naps but he slept over an hour. When he woke, her cheek was in the curve of his shoulder and she was snoring lightly. He eased out from under, careful not to do anything that would wake her. In a few minutes he was dressed and bent for the bottle.

No, he decided, he'd leave the rest for her. His way of saying thanks.

The glare of the sun made him squint. He should have waited for his eyes to adjust but he didn't and he paid for his mistake.

As he was reaching for the reins a hard object was jammed against his spine. He didn't need to guess what it was.

A gun hammer clicked.

18

Fargo looked over his shoulder. There was a tall one and a short one and both held six-shooters. They were as unremarkable as dirt. "I don't have any money," he lied. He took them for holdup men.

"Who the hell cares?" the tall one said. He had corncob hair and a mustache and a small scar at the corner of his mouth.

"You're stealing my horse?" Fargo would laugh if they were. Twice in less than one week was too damn silly for words.

"Listen to him," the short one said. He had a voice so low, he croaked like a bullfrog. "Jumps to conclusions, don't he?"

"You didn't notice us but we came in the saloon while you were shooting the shit out of that homesteader," the tall one said. "We work for Ransom Trayburn."

Suddenly it was deadly serious. "You don't say," Fargo said.

"We do," Bullfrog croaked. "And it struck us that we'd be doing our boss a favor by not letting you go after him."

"One of the things he pays us to do is keep nuisances away," Tall Man said.

"And you look to be a hell of a nuisance," Bullfrog remarked.

"We figure to nip you in the bud," Tall Man said, and smirked, "with lead poisoning."

Fargo said, "The easy thing would be for him to give back my horse."

Tall Man shook his head. "That's not going to happen. Once Mr. Trayburn buys a horse, it's his."

Bullfrog nodded. "Besides, he had no way of knowing that Pulanski stole that stallion."

"As far as he was concerned, the horse belonged to the homesteader," Tall Man said.

"Which brings us back to our problem," Bullfrog said. "What to do about you?"

"There are two ways this can go," Tall Man said. "You can give us your word that you'll leave the territory and never try to get your horse back—"

"And we'd be stupid as hell to believe you," Bullfrog said.

"—or we can make sure you don't become a nuisance by taking you off into the woods and doing what folks usually do with nuisances," Tall Man finished.

"There's a third way," Fargo said.

Both appeared puzzled and Bullfrog croaked, "Oh? Suppose you explain it."

"It's where my brother shoots both of you in the leg and we have a long talk about Ransom Trayburn and stolen horses and such."

"Your brother?" Bullfrog said.

Fargo looked past them and smiled and said, "You can get to shooting now."

It was the oldest trick in the hills. But he said it so naturally and sincerely, they were fooled. Both gun hands turned their heads, and in that instant, Fargo exploded into action. He sidestepped and whirled and drew and smashed the Colt's barrel against Tall Man's jaw. It staggered Tall Man, and his gun drooped.

Bullfrog must have seen it out of the corner of his eye because he fired from the hip before he'd turned his head. But as he squeezed off the shot, Fargo moved.

Bullfrog missed.

Fargo didn't. He fanned a shot that jolted Bullfrog just as Bullfrog fired again. The slug intended for Fargo caught Tall Man low in the back and both of them went down, Tall Man onto his belly and Bullfrog onto his back. Bullfrog tried to take aim.

Fargo fired. Bullfrog bucked and yowled and extended his revolver with both hands, and Fargo gave him a third nostril.

Tall Man had dropped his pistol and was twitching from the waist up. From the waist down he was perfectly still.

Fargo kicked the six-gun out of reach and rolled him over.

"I can't feel my legs," Tall Man said.

"You can feel the rest of you." Fargo pressed the Colt to Tall Man's gut. "They say a belly wound hurts worse than anything."

"You son of a bitch."

"I want to know about your boss," Fargo said. "I want to know what he does with the horses he buys."

"Go to hell."

There were hollers in the saloon and a commotion and the tramp of running feet.

Fargo ignored the ruckus. "Tell me what I want to know and this will go easier."

"I'm no weak sister."

"Where does Trayburn take the horses? What does he do with them?"

"He eats them," Tall Man said, and uttered a vicious laugh.

"You get one more chance."

"He feeds them to his dogs."

"Suit yourself," Fargo said. He thumbed back the hammer just as people from the saloon came rushing around the corner and lurched to a stop in consternation.

"What's going on here?" someone demanded.

"Don't tell us you're at it again?" another said. It sounded like Jiggs.

Tall Man did more twitching. "You'll never see that horse of yours again. I can die happy knowing that."

"Die then," Fargo said.

At the boom of the Colt, Tall Man threw back his head and seemed to scream soundlessly at the sky. Then he went limp.

"Sweet Jesus," a man exclaimed. "You're a killing fiend."

Fargo straightened and began to reload. "They worked for Trayburn."

"We know," Jiggs said. "He has upwards of twenty more just like them."

"Trayburn will be after you now," another remarked.

"That's good," Fargo said, "because I'll be after him."

"This is no joking matter, mister."

Fargo stared at the speaker. "It sure as hell isn't."

"Why die for a horse?"

"You have another right there," noticed a man behind Jiggs.

Fargo twirled the Colt into his holster and stepped to the roan and climbed on. He saw Holly in the doorway, her hair disheveled, and nodded.

"Wait," someone called out. "What about the bodies?"

"Bury them or let them rot." Fargo went to rein around.

"Mister, you have a lot of bark on you. But so do Trayburn and his gun hands. Give it up while you still can."

"Not in this life or any other."

"Word will get to him. He'll be ready for you."

Fargo had dallied long enough. He tapped his spurs. At the first bend in the trail he looked back. They were still there, staring.

Holly smiled and blew him a kiss.

Fargo didn't return the favor. He had one thing and one thing only on his mind.

It involved spilling a lot more blood.

19

Every time Fargo set eyes on Denver it had grown by leaps and more than a few bounds.

Born out of the greed of the gold rush, the city bustled with vim and vigor. It also nearly burst at the seams with violence.

Just the year before, the killings and the thievery reached the point where a vigilante group formed. Lawbreakers were given a choice: leave the territory or be summarily hanged.

Still, the wildness persisted. The churchgoing element came up with a way to contain it by allowing those who liked to indulge in what the churchgoing crowd called vices to do so in a part of the city that some had taken to calling Hell on Earth.

Originally it was along Cherry Creek, west of Larimer Street. As the city spread, so did the rowdy district. Gambling dens and bawdy houses were sprouting faster than houses of worship.

And just as there were gold barons and cattle barons, Denver had its own particular breed of another kind: pleasure barons. Men who owned a string of flesh and greed pits.

Men like Ransom Trayburn. One of the first to see the potential to Denver's dark side, Trayburn owned more saloons, whorehouses and gambling dives than anyone.

He was well on his way to being the richest man west of the Mississippi.

All this Fargo learned from casual talks with barkeeps the evening he arrived. All he had to do was mention how the city was growing and that he'd heard some men were making money hand over fist, and let drop Trayburn's name.

Try as he might, though, Fargo couldn't find out where

79

Trayburn lived, or whether Trayburn had a stable where he kept his horses.

It turned out to be common knowledge that Trayburn had been buying horses for some time. No one had any idea what he did with them. It was assumed he must have a stud farm. Horse breeding was profitable. But when Fargo asked, no one could recollect ever hearing of Trayburn selling a horse. All he ever did was buy them.

It was damned frustrating, and didn't improve Fargo's mood any.

Along about midnight he decided to find a place to bed down. A good night's sleep and he'd start out fresh, and so help him, he'd get the answers he needed before the next day was out.

Fargo tried not to think about the Ovaro. Anything could have happened to it. Then again, no one paid top dollar for a horse to let it come to harm. He told himself that wherever the Ovaro was, it was probably being well looked after. He told himself that a lot to keep his worse imaginings at bay.

He'd asked at the last saloon he visited and the bartender told him to try a boardinghouse on Howard Street.

The barman himself stayed there. "It's clean and reasonable and the gal who runs it is a looker."

Fargo was dubious about pounding on the door so late but the barkeep said not to worry, that the lady took in boarders at any hour of the day or night.

Howard Street was just outside the red light district. It intersected with Kull Boulevard at one end and Solomon Avenue at the other.

Fargo tied the roan at a hitch rail out front, opened a gate, and walked up a gravel path to a wide porch. A small lamp was set in a recess above the door, apparently so anyone returning late wouldn't have to fumble for their key. He knocked, lightly. When no one came he knocked again, louder. When that failed, he shrugged and turned to go and was at the steps when the door opened and a sultry voice said, "May I help you?"

Most boardinghouse matrons were old and as broad as buckboards. Not this one. She wasn't much past thirty and she had a shape an hourglass would envy. Not even the robe she was bundled in could hide her abundant charms. She had red hair and red lips and eyes as blue as his. "Are you catching moths?" she asked, and grinned.

Fargo hadn't realized his mouth was hanging open. He closed it and coughed. "I was told you might have a room to let."

"How long would you need it for?"

"I'm not rightly sure."

"What are you doing in Denver?"

Fargo cocked his head. "No offense, ma'am, but I don't see where that's any of your business."

"I beg to disagree," she said pleasantly. "I don't let just anyone stay here. If you're partial to drink and rowdiness and womanizing, I'd suggest you find someplace else."

Now it was Fargo who grinned. "I'm partial to all three. But I won't do any of it here if it's against your rules."

"I have your word?"

"You do."

"Good." She nodded and stepped back and held the door for him. "You may enter."

Fargo caught a whiff of lilac water as he moved past. "You're awful trusting."

"You think so?" She took her other hand out of her robe's pocket; she was holding a derringer.

"So if I sneak a drink you'll shoot me?"

"Try it and find out." She laughed and closed the door. "I'm Phoebe Mavins, by the way. You can call me Miss Mavins."

"I was thinking of calling you 'easy on the eyes.'"

"None of that," Phoebe said, but she was smiling. "I know there are boardinghouses that are run more like brothels but mine isn't one of them. I gave all that up to become respectable."

"You don't say."

"I do," Phoebe said. "I worked the line back when Denver wasn't more than cabins and tents. I saved every cent, enough that when an elderly gentleman friend died and graciously left me a small amount for all the pleasure I'd given him, between that and my nest egg I had the down payment for this." She motioned at the walls and ceiling.

Her mention of being one of the first made Fargo think of

what a barkeep had told him. "You must have got here about the same time as Ransom Trayburn."

Phoebe's smile faded. "What made you mention him?"

"I'm trying to find him."

"Trayburn is very wealthy and very dangerous," Phoebe said. "What do you want with him, if you don't mind my asking?"

"It's about a horse," Fargo hedged. He'd had time to think on the ride from Estes Park and decided it wouldn't do to tear through Denver like a mad bull in a china shop. He'd draw too much of the wrong attention. Word would reach Trayburn and Trayburn would set more gun hands on him. He needed to work this smartly or he might never set eyes on the Ovaro again.

"Oh," Phoebe said. "You're one of those."

"If I am it's news to me."

"You must be a rider. Those who do the betting are usually rolling in money and, if you won't mind my saying, you don't strike me as having more than you know what to do with."

"I'm a rider," Fargo lied in the hope she would reveal more.

A look of disgust came over her. "That's too bad. You're easy on the eyes but I won't have any truck with someone who does what you do. I happen to like horses."

"So do I."

"How can you, and let that happen to them?" Phoebe headed down the hall. "Follow me. I'll show you to your room."

Fargo mulled how to find out more. If he said the wrong thing she might become suspicious and imitate a clam. He played it safe by asking, "How is it you know about the horses?"

"I have a client to thank," Phoebe said. "One of my last before I gave up the sheets. He breezed into town for one of Trayburn's spectacles and took me along. Only those he invites are allowed to attend. They can bring a guest if they want, and Trayburn makes it a point to explain what will happen to them if they tell anyone."

"Why do you call them spectacles?"

"That's what Trayburn calls them and it fits. The bears.

The wolves. The Indians. The rest of it. Those poor horses don't stand a prayer."

Fargo had no notion what she was talking about but it spiked his worry for the Ovaro. So much so, he asked without thinking, "Are you saying he has the horses fight bears and wolves?"

Phoebe stopped. "I thought you said you're a rider."

Grasping at a straw, Fargo said, "This is my first time."

"It could well be your last." Phoebe moved to a junction and turned down the right-hand hall to the last room on the left and opened the door. "This is yours."

Fargo took a gamble. "Why my last?"

In the act of lighting a lamp, Phoebe gave him a sharp glance. "Didn't they tell you *anything*?" She shook her head. "No. I suppose they wouldn't. It's such a big secret. And Trayburn makes everyone promise not to say a word about it, or else."

"I'd be grateful for anything you saw fit to tell me," Fargo fished.

"It's vile, is what it is," Phoebe said. "You must be a good rider. But it sounds like they didn't tell you that a lot of the riders get hurt and some are killed. For the horses it's even worse."

"No one told me, no."

"Figures." Phoebe set the lamp on the table. "If you had any sense you'd light a shuck before Trayburn finds out you're here. But you're probably like the rest and figure it can't happen to you."

"What can't?" Fargo asked.

"Why, you dying, of course."

20

Fargo mulled over all he'd learned while wending his way on foot along Denver's busy streets after leaving the Grand Saloon. It was owned by Ransom Trayburn. So were the Grand Hotel, the Grand Dance Hall and the Grand Social Club. That last made Fargo shake his head. People came up with the fanciest names for whorehouses.

Trayburn had his fingers in other business, but from what Fargo was told, all the *Grands* were the ones Trayburn personally ran and spent time at.

It was a barkeep at the Grand Saloon who mentioned that Trayburn did, in fact, have a ranch somewhere, but the barkeep had no idea where.

Fargo had spent the whole day going from Grand this to Grand that, and the tidbit about the ranch was all he learned.

Now, tired and disappointed and more worried about the Ovaro than ever, he bent his boots to the boardinghouse. At that hour all the other boarders appeared to be in bed. Every window was dark save for a light in the kitchen.

On an impulse he went down the hall, and who should he find seated at the kitchen table drinking tea but the lady of the house.

"Ma'am."

Phoebe had heard his spurs. "Did you find your employer?" she asked. "Did he explain how things are with his despicable races?"

Fargo pulled out the chair across from her and sat. He came to a decision. "I'm going to lay my cards on the table."

"How so?" Phoebe asked. She didn't sound all that interested. In fact, her tone was tinged with scorn.

"I lied to you."

Phoebe set her cup on the saucer and eyed him critically. "I despise liars. What, exactly, did you lie about? And why are you admitting it to me?"

Fargo gave it to her sort of straight. He left out the part about Carrie and the Pulanskis and left in the part about the Ovaro being taken and how he believed the stallion had been sold to Ransom Trayburn. "I'm trying to find him and I don't know who I can trust. So . . ." He stopped and shrugged.

Phoebe studied him for an uncomfortably long time. "So you lied to me, not knowing if you could trust me? I think you're telling the truth." She stopped. "This horse must mean a lot to you."

"You don't know the half of it."

"I feel sorry for you," Phoebe said. "You'll never see your animal again."

"Like hell."

"If your horse has been picked to take part in Trayburn's Grand Race, as he calls it, he'll have it out at his ranch. But no one knows where it is. Not even me, and I've been there."

"How is that possible?" Fargo asked.

"It works like this," Phoebe said. "The guests are driven to the race in special carriages with the windows covered. You can't look out to see where you are even if you want to. I know. I was curious and I tried. All I can tell you is that by my best reckoning, the ranch is six hours or so east of Denver. At least, that's how long it took to get there."

"Goddamn it," Fargo said in frustration. He bowed his head and sighed. "Tell me more about the races, then."

"Spectacles, remember?" Phoebe gave a slight shudder. "They're not run on a racetrack, as you'd expect. There's this canyon. It's about a mile long, with cliffs on both sides. The riders start at one end and try to make it alive to the other."

"You said something about bears and wolves."

Phoebe nodded. "Ransom has them caught up in the mountains and brought there. He keeps them half starved and lets them loose in the canyon the day of the race. Rattlesnakes, too, I was told. Now and then he throws in some Indians."

"Why would they take part?"

"My escort let it drop that Trayburn finds tame ones who

have fallen into the bottle and can't climb out. He offers them all the whiskey they can drink to put arrows into the riders."

"I've never heard the like," Fargo admitted.

"I told you they're spectacles. But that's Trayburn for you. When you meet him, you'll understand. He never does anything by halves."

Fargo imagined the Ovaro being forced to run a race like that and almost did some shuddering of his own. "I have to find his ranch."

"Good luck." Phoebe toyed with her cup, then said, "Maybe the best way is to go on pretending that you're a rider. Let it be known that you want to ride in a race. Word might reach him. He's always looking for men and horses. Some riders bring their own but Trayburn supplies horses to those who don't have good mounts."

"I'm obliged."

"Save your thanks. My advice might get you killed." Phoebe reached across and placed her hand on his. "Now that I know how you really are, I wouldn't want that."

Fargo looked her in the eyes. "Any chance you'd like some company tonight?"

"Listen to you. Just because I'm being nice doesn't mean I want to part my legs for you. I told you. I gave that up."

"You're a nun and you're keeping it a secret?"

"You think you know women—is that it?"

"I know I like to fuck."

"Don't be crude," Phoebe said, and pulled her hand away.

"It was a compliment."

"Talking like that to a lady you hardly know? How is that flattering?"

"I don't offer to go to bed with every woman I meet. I have my standards."

"This should be good," Phoebe said. "What are they?"

"She has to be under seventy."

Phoebe laughed. "You, handsome, are a cad."

"And she has to have a nose."

Phoebe went on laughing.

"Tits help, but they don't have to be watermelons."

"Stop."

"I like them to have teeth, too. Which is why they have to be under seventy."

"Please stop." Phoebe was holding her side.

"Toes aren't important although now and then I like to suck on them."

Phoebe gasped and shook her head. "Damn you. I hurt."

"Did I mention ears?"

Phoebe laughed herself out and sat back and sucked in deep breaths. "That sure struck my funny bone."

"So yes or no?"

"Not tonight," Phoebe replied, but her face softened. "Some night soon, maybe. If you're as much fun in bed as you are at the table, it will be worth it."

"I can tickle you if you like to laugh while you're being poked."

"Goodness, you're something."

Fargo smiled. For a minute there, she'd taken his mind off the Ovaro.

"I've got to ask," Phoebe said. "Let's say you find your horse. What then? Do you ride off and let it drop? Or do you aim to raise some hell with Ransom Trayburn?"

"I aim to raise a whole lot of hell," Fargo said.

21

The next day Fargo strode into the Grand Saloon shortly before noon. He bought a bottle and sat in on a poker game and spent the next several hours winning a little and losing less. He wasn't much interested in the cards. From where he sat he could see the whole length of the bar and the batwings and the doors that led to rooms at the back. He figured that sooner or later Ransom Trayburn would show up.

Along about five, Kiley Strake sauntered in. A lot of the patrons stopped what they were doing to stare, which said a lot about Strake's reputation.

The batwings had barely stopped swinging when someone else entered, and everything stopped.

Ransom Trayburn. It had to be. He was taller than Fargo and broader across the shoulders and wore a tailored suit that most folks could only dream of owning.

Curly blond hair framed a face that was remarkable for a long scar on the right cheek, and for the icy gleam in Trayburn's piercing green eyes. It could be Fargo's imagination, but he got the notion that Ransom Trayburn looked down his nose at the world and everyone in it.

The drinkers at the bar quickly moved aside. Strake stood with his back to it and said, "A drink for Mr. Trayburn. The usual."

A barkeep scurried to obey.

Ransom Trayburn walked to a table in the far corner. Fargo had noticed earlier that it was the only empty table in the saloon, and kept that way. Now he knew why. It was reserved for the big man.

The batwings parted yet again and half a dozen gun hands

89

trailed their boss in. They spread out around the table as Strake brought a bottle and a glass over.

Here was Fargo's chance. He'd reckoned to try Phoebe's idea but he couldn't very well go strolling over with Strake there. Strake had seen him at the Pulanski place.

"Damn," he said out loud.

"What was that?" one of the players asked. "What are you upset about, mister?"

"Nothing," Fargo said gruffly. He didn't dare let Strake see him or he could forget posing as a rider. But what to do? he asked himself. There was only one answer.

It looked as if Trayburn aimed to stay a while. Strake had taken a seat with his back to a wall so he could survey the entire saloon.

Fargo needed to get out of there. As luck would have it, several men peeled from the bar and made for the batwings. They'd pass close to his table. He told the other players he was folding and rose, his shoulders hunched to hide his height.

He timed it just right. The townsmen were between him and Strake when he stepped in front of them and headed out. They paid him no mind, and neither, he was relieved to see when he glanced back, did Strake.

It was getting late and most businesses would close soon. The first general store he came to, Fargo turned in and walked over to a section devoted to men's clothes. Normally he wouldn't be caught dead in store-bought duds but it was the best disguise he could think of.

"May I help you, sir?" a heavy man in an apron asked.

"I need a shirt and pants and a hat," Fargo said, frowning.

"You don't seem very happy about it."

"Is this all you have?"

Now it was the man who frowned. "I'll have you know I carry one of the best selections in Denver. Work and dress shirts. Pants for the farm or the city. And hats of all kinds." He gestured at a nearby rack.

Fargo stepped to it. There were bowlers and derbies. There were the floppy hats that farmers wore. There was a hat a cowboy would wear. But absolutely none that wouldn't feel as out of place on his head as a crow's nest. "Hell," he said.

"Now you don't like my hats?"

"This was a bad idea," Fargo realized. New clothes couldn't disguise his height or build. And what about his beard? The only way to disguise that was to cut it off, and he'd be damned if he would. "Son of a bitch."

"Do you mean me?"

"No."

"Are you cussing for the fun of it or are you drunk?" The man sniffed a few times. "I don't smell liquor on your breath."

"I reckon I'll have to do this the hard way."

"Do what? Buy clothes? It's easy as anything. You pick what you want and you pay and leave."

"Thanks for your help." Fargo turned.

"Wait. Now you're not buying clothes? Mister, you have me confused as hell."

"Forget I was here."

"I'll try. But you're mighty strange."

Fargo stood under the overhang outside and cursed himself for a dunce. He was no playactor. For him to try to infiltrate Trayburn's outfit like some kind of spy was just plain ridiculous. There was only one way to go about it. The way he went about everything.

Squaring his shoulders, Fargo returned to the Grand Saloon. He slammed into the batwings and they crashed against the wall, causing everyone in earshot to give a start or glance over.

Fargo shoved two men who were watching a card game out of his way. One squawked and the other cocked his fist but took one look and lowered it again.

The commotion had drawn the interest of Trayburn's ring of protectors.

Fargo made straight for the corner table.

A gun hand with carrot hair and peach fuzz on his chin moved to block him, saying, "Hold up, mister. What do you think you're doing?"

Fargo gave him no warning. He slicked the Colt and slammed the barrel against the kid's chin, and carrot-top folded like so much limp paper. In the same motion Fargo twirled the Colt back into his holster. Another couple of steps and he stopped and planted himself.

Kiley Strake uncoiled out of his chair like a rattler about to strike. His hands were poised but he glanced at his employer as if he had to get approval first.

Ransom Trayburn showed no worry whatsoever. As calmly as could be, he sipped some Scotch and said, "What do we have here?"

"You have one pissed-off son of a bitch," Fargo said.

22

Ransom Trayburn was as ruffled as a rock. He put his glass down and tilted his head and regarded Fargo with what Fargo would swear was amusement. "Red won't like you walloping him like that."

"I don't give a good damn what Red does and doesn't like," Fargo said. "I want my horse and I want him now."

"Why come to me?"

"It would be a mistake to take me for stupid," Fargo said.

Kiley Strake broke in with, "Boss, I remember this hombre. He was at the Pulanski place."

"Harold stole my horse and sold it to you," Fargo said to Trayburn. "For the last time, I want it back."

"Ah," Trayburn said, and surprised Fargo by indicating an empty chair. "Have a seat and we'll talk this out like gentlemen."

"There's nothing to jaw about."

"Says you," Trayburn said. "But I paid—" He glanced at Strake. "How much was it again?"

"A thousand dollars."

"That's right. I paid Harold Pulanski a thousand dollars for a horse he claimed was his. And now you want me to hand it over on your say-so that it's yours?" Trayburn's scar twitched. "Do you have proof?"

"I don't carry a goddamned bill of sale around with me."

"That's too bad. Because now it's your word against his. I suppose I'll have to send for him and the three of us can hash it out."

"He can't do much hashing," Fargo said, "unless dead men can talk."

"You killed him?" Trayburn said, and laughed.

"And two of your quick-draw artists who weren't so quick."

Trayburn's mirth died. "Are we missing anyone?" he said to Strake without looking at him.

"Lute and Branham were supposed to be back from Estes Park last night but never showed."

"Well, now," Trayburn said, and his green eyes glittered. "They weren't infants. Who are you, mister?"

Fargo told him.

"Heard of you," Trayburn said after a moment, and the strangest expression came over him. He smiled and said, "Please. Take a seat. This puts a whole new complexion on things."

Fargo was surprised by the friendly smile. He glanced at the ring of protectors and Trayburn immediately shifted in his chair to say, "Boys, there'll be no gunplay. This man is not to be harmed. Anyone who tries answers to me. And you know what that means."

Apparently they did because they retreated to the wall. Some of them glared at Fargo. The news about Lute and Branham had them mad.

Fargo hooked the chair with his boot and pulled it out farther. He turned it and straddled it so he was face on to Kiley Strake, the most dangerous of the bunch. Then it occurred to him that he'd never seen Trayburn use a pistol, or heard a word about whether he was quick or slow. All folks said was that you never, ever crossed him. Which made him wonder if Trayburn might be as dangerous as Strake.

"You study things," Ransom Trayburn said. "I admire that. I study on things myself."

"We're not blood brothers," Fargo said.

"We're not enemies, either, unless you want us to be," Trayburn said with that annoying calmness. "It wasn't me who stole your horse. I bought it from Pulanski in good faith."

"Noble of you."

Instead of being insulted, Trayburn chuckled. "You bite down and don't let go. I admire that, too. But the truth is, Pulanski showed up as I was about to leave Estes to come back to Denver. He'd about ridden his own horse into the ground. He said he knew that I'd sent Kiley to his place, and he wanted to make good on the debt he owed me, and would I take a look at a horse he'd come into and was it worth anything to me."

Kiley Strake threw in, "That's exactly how it was. I'd seen the horse in Pulanski's corral, and mentioned that to Mr. Trayburn."

Fargo supposed they could be telling the truth. How were they to know the Ovaro was his?

"The dirt farmer even had a bill of sale," Trayburn said. "As a matter of fact . . ." He slid a hand inside his jacket and Fargo flicked his hand to his Colt. Trayburn chuckled and said, "Quick hands." He pulled out a leather billfold. Opening it, Trayburn thumbed through a lot of bills and folded pieces of paper, saying, "I haven't been back all that long and I believe I still have it with me. Ah. Here we go." He held out a piece that looked as if it had been torn from a tablet. "See for yourself."

The scribble was hard to read. It was short and to the point, *"Sold my horse for five hundred dollars to Harold Pulanski."* It was signed *"Rufus Crone"* and dated a month and a half ago.

"Harold wrote this himself and came up with the name to trick you," Fargo guessed.

"I was suspicious," Trayburn said. "A man like him, with a horse like that. He wouldn't have known good horseflesh if the horse bit him on the ass." Trayburn paused. "And that Ovaro is about the finest animal I've ever set eyes on."

"My animal," Fargo said.

"I believe that now, yes."

"You do?"

"What was it you said to me a bit ago?" Trayburn rejoined. "Oh. Yes." His eyes narrowed. "It wouldn't do to take me for stupid."

"I want him back," Fargo said.

"And you shall have him," Trayburn replied.

"Just like that? No fight? No fuss?"

"What purpose would that serve?"

"You'll be out a thousand dollars."

Trayburn motioned at the saloon. "On good nights I make that much in an hour at this establishment alone. And in case you haven't heard, I have other businesses that bring in just as much, and more. To me a thousand dollars is no more than a dollar is to you."

"So, you're just going to hand him over to me?"

"I am," Trayburn assured him.

"Well, hell," Fargo said.

23

Fargo hadn't expected Ransom Trayburn to be so reasonable. After all the things he'd heard, he'd reckoned he'd have to spill blood to get the Ovaro back. "I didn't think it would be this easy," he admitted.

"I'm a businessman," Trayburn said. "I know when to cut my losses. And besides, I did say I've heard of you. Several newspaper accounts, as I recollect. It seems you've shot a lot of people."

"Well, hell," Fargo said again.

"Mr. Strake, here, has shot a lot of people, too. But he doesn't get into the newspaper nearly as much. You should share your secret."

"My secret is that I don't want them to write about me but the peckerwoods do it anyway. And they don't always get it right."

"Journalists never let the facts get in the way of their stories," Trayburn said. "I've had some things written about me, not all of it flattering. It's led me to the conclusion that all writers are liars. The good ones will say so. The rest have their heads so far up their asses, they don't hear their own lies."

Fargo couldn't help laughing.

"Now as to your horse," Trayburn said, "I don't see many Ovaros. Not around here, anyway. I understand they're more common down along the border country."

"Where is he? I'll go fetch him."

"I'm afraid that's not possible."

Fargo was instantly suspicious. "So much for handing him right over."

"I would if I could," Trayburn said. "But the truth is, he's not here."

"Goddamn it."

"I have a ranch a considerable piece northeast of Denver. I sent him on ahead as I would any horse I buy. I'm not trying to renege or trick you. You're welcome to come with me and claim him."

"I am?"

"Why do you sound so surprised?"

"I'd heard that you keep your ranch a secret," Fargo said.

"You, of all people, should know not to believe everything you hear," Trayburn said. "People love to gossip." He paused. "I don't go around telling everyone where it is, and why the hell should I? I like my privacy. And why invite trouble when my stock would give a horse thief wet dreams?"

"Makes sense," Fargo said.

"I leave in the morning. You can accompany us, if you like."

"In one of your special carriages with no windows?"

"Heard about those, have you?" Trayburn said, and grinned. "I hold races from time to time. One is coming up, in fact. That's how my guests are brought. But again, it's to safeguard my privacy and protect my animals. I have no need of that with you. You can ride whatever you are using at the moment."

"You don't care that I'll know where your ranch is?"

"Why should I? None of the newspaper accounts said you're a horse thief. Or have you taken up a new calling?"

Fargo snorted, and had a thought. "What about your two gun hands?"

"What about them? The pair in Estes Park braced you on their own account. I can hire men to replace them just like that." Trayburn snapped his fingers.

"I have to ask," Fargo said. "Folks say your races aren't really races. That you throw in wolves and bears and more."

"Preposterous," Trayburn said. "Do you honestly think that someone who loves good horseflesh as much as I do, who paid a thousand dollars for your Ovaro and has paid a lot more than that for others, would put them in peril?"

It did seem preposterous. But Fargo had no reason to suspect Phoebe made it up.

Trayburn was shaking his head. "The horses at my ranch are well treated. Better so than at most ranches, I daresay."

"That's good to hear," Fargo said. The Ovaro would be well taken care of until he got there.

"You still haven't said. Is it yes or is it no?"

"Do you even have to ask? I'd go through hell for that horse."

"Would you, indeed?" Trayburn said. "It's rare to find someone so devoted to his mount."

Fargo had met more than a few cowhands and others who were as fond of their horses as he was of the Ovaro. "You must not get out much."

"If I sleep in the same bed two nights in a row, it's unusual," Trayburn said. "Be in front of the Grand Hotel at eight tomorrow morning. We'll head out from there." He stood. "Now, if you'll excuse me, I have other matters to attend to."

The hired guns closed in and formed a phalanx around him. Red had recovered, and glowered.

Kiley Strake was the last to depart. He paused near Fargo's chair and said, "Craig Lute was my pard."

"Was he the tall one or frog voice?" Fargo said.

"Frog," Strake said. "We hooked up five years ago. It's too bad Mr. Trayburn is bending over backwards for you. I'd like to do to you as you did to Lute."

"You'd try," Fargo said.

"Just so you know. If Mr. Trayburn changes his mind about you, I'll come after you, and I'll be on the prod."

"Thanks for the warning."

"You won't feel so grateful with lead in you." Strake placed his hand on his pearl-handled Remington. "For two bits I'd do you now."

Fargo fished out a coin and tossed it on the table. "Start the dance." For an instant he thought Strake would. But no, the shootist shook his head and strolled off with a last taunt over his shoulder.

"Be careful what you wish for, mister."

All Fargo wished for was the Ovaro. That his run-in with Ransom Trayburn had gone so smoothly bothered him. It was his experience that when things were too easy, he should take that as an omen that worse was yet to come.

24

"I was telling the truth, consarn you," Phoebe said heatedly. "Call me a liar again and I'll scratch your eyes out."

They were at her table in the kitchen. Fargo had returned thinking to get a good night's sleep and she informed him she had supper waiting. He told her she shouldn't have but she took him by the arm and hustled him down the hall, and here they were.

"I don't care what Trayburn claims," she went on. "You can believe him or you can believe me but I don't want to hear it if you don't believe me."

Fargo forked a piece of pork chop into his mouth. She'd also whipped up potatoes with gravy, and peas. A plate of sliced bread and a butter dish were to one side.

"You don't believe him, do you?" Phoebe asked, sounding hurt.

"He's too slick by half," Fargo said.

"I saw what I saw that day," Phoebe insisted. "Naturally he's not going to admit it. Besides, you said he'd heard of you. It could be he doesn't want to draw the attention of your friends by harming you."

Fargo hadn't thought of that. Not that he had all that many friends.

"You be careful, you hear? Don't turn your back to him if you can help it."

"I'll be on my guard," Fargo said, and bit into a piece of bread. He'd need eyes in the back of his head to watch Strake and all those kill-for-hires but he wasn't about to change his mind.

"Anyway," Phoebe said sulkily, "I didn't go to all

this bother for us to argue. I've been thinking your offer over."

"I made an offer?" Fargo said in mock innocence.

"You damn well know you did," Phoebe retorted. "And I'd like to take you up on it."

Suddenly Fargo understood why she was so gussied up. She'd done her hair and had on a dress more fitting for a dance hall than house chores. "Would you, now?"

"Don't smirk like that. It doesn't become you."

"It's the only smirk I know how to do."

Phoebe laughed, and the tension between them faded. "After we eat there's dessert."

Fargo stared at the fine swell of her bosom. "Right there is all the dessert I need."

"That's more like it," Phoebe said, and wriggled girlishly so that her breasts jiggled.

So much for turning in early, Fargo thought. He dipped the bread in the gravy and savored each chew.

"I never saw a man who likes to eat so much," Phoebe remarked.

"Wait until you see me between your legs."

She burst out in more laughter and her jugs did more jiggling. "I'm looking forward to this."

So was Fargo. It would take his mind off the Ovaro and the problem he faced if she was right and Ransom Trayburn was lying through his perfect teeth.

"You don't want a slice of pie, then? It's peach. A friend of mine, a farmer's wife, gave me some of her preserves a while back."

"Bring a slice to the bedroom," Fargo suggested.

"What on earth for?"

"You'll see."

Fargo took his time eating. They had all night. He caught Phoebe eyeing him now and again. She was eager for him to get done and kept fidgeting.

"You know," she commented at one point, "you're taking an awful chance going to Trayburn's ranch. Once you're there you'll be at his mercy."

"And he'll be at mine," Fargo said.

"I was there, remember? He has gun sharks all over the place. You can't go for a stroll without one of them latching on to you."

"I don't expect it to be a cakewalk."

"If you make it back alive no one will be happier than me but I'm not counting on it."

"Be careful," Fargo said. "You might build my confidence too high."

Phoebe went to the counter and came back with the peach pie and a small plate and a carving knife. She cut the pie into sections and lifted a triangle onto the plate. She sniffed the piece and said, "Makes my mouth water."

Fargo stared at her ass. "Mine too." He ate the pie and and drained the last of his coffee.

"Would you care for more of anything?"

Fargo stared at the junction of her thighs. "I do but it's not food."

"Oh my."

Phoebe stacked the dirty dishes and left the pots and pans on the stove and came over and took his hand.

"Want something?" Fargo said.

"I have a nice soft bed waiting." She tried to pull him out of the chair.

"Do you, now?" Suddenly standing, Fargo clasped her hard against him and molded his mouth to hers. Her lips parted and her tongue met his. She groaned when he cupped her bottom. She gasped when he scooped her off her feet, turned, and placed her on her back on the table.

"What in the world . . . ?"

Fargo cupped a tit and squeezed and she writhed and kissed his neck and his ear. He cupped her other tit and pinched both nipples through her dress. Her legs rose and wrapped around him and she began to pry at his belt buckle.

"God, I want you in me."

"Not so fast."

"What? Why not?" Phoebe said, and then she saw the piece of peach pie he had saved in his hand. "What are you fixing to do with that?"

"You can't guess?" Fargo hiked at her dress and the chemise she had on underneath, sliding them above her knees and then her thighs and her hips. He held the slice so she could see what he was about to do.

"You wouldn't," Phoebe gasped.

Fargo did.

25

The Grand Hotel lived up to its name. The doors were gilded in bronze and there was a doorman in a purple uniform. A sign on the roof that could be seen from a quarter mile away was in cursive, and it was one of the tallest buildings in the growing city.

None of which Fargo gave a damn about. All he had on his mind was the Ovaro. He got to the hotel twenty minutes early and drew rein down the block.

The hotel didn't surprise him, given Ransom Trayburn's taste for elegance. Five equally elegant carriages were parked in front. They had canvas over the windows so no one could see in or out.

A large group of obviously well-to-do men and women was gathering. The men with flashy stickpins and gold chains for their watches, and canes. The women were in bright dresses with a lot of lace and frills, and hats that only women would wear.

Also present and lounging about but plainly there to see that no one bothered the rich crowd were a number of two-legged wolves with revolvers high on their hips or worn for a cross-draw.

At about five minutes to eight, Ransom Trayburn strolled out of the hotel with Kiley Strake and more protectors in his wake. Red, the man Fargo had struck with his Colt in the saloon, was one of them.

Only then did Fargo gig the roan.

Trayburn greeted him with a smile and a bob of his head. "You're right on time."

"What's this?" Fargo said, with a bob of his own at the carriages and the well-to-dos.

"I told you that I had a race coming up."

Fargo recollected that he had, in fact. Trayburn just hadn't said how soon. "How long will it take to get to this ranch of yours?"

Trayburn gazed at the bright clear sky. "On a fine day like today, about six hours."

That fit with what Phoebe had told Fargo and lent more weight to the rest of what she'd told him. "That's a far piece."

"Hell," Trayburn said. "It takes longer to get to Estes Park." He, too, was carrying a cane, and he twirled it and leaned on it and said, "You must be chomping at the bit to reclaim that fine horse of yours."

"You have no idea," Fargo said.

"I don't blame you. Most people don't realize how special an animal like that is. To them a horse is just a horse. We know better."

"When did you become such a horse lover?" Fargo asked out of idle curiosity.

"When I saw my first horse race. I was twelve, and my father took me. It was in Kansas City. He let me place a bet." Trayburn's face lit at the memory. "I'll never forget the excitement I felt. I leaned on the rail and shouted for my horse to win, and damned if he didn't. It was only a couple of dollars but I was hooked from that day on." He paused. "Do you feel that way about anything?"

"Poker," Fargo said, "and poking."

"Then you know. Sometimes we like a thing so much, we can't do without it."

Fargo hated to admit it but he felt a certain kinship with the man. Annoyed at himself, he looked at the carriages. "How do they breathe in there, anyhow?"

"Airholes in top," Trayburn revealed. "You should see inside. Here, let me show you."

They stepped to the first one and Trayburn gestured at the driver who quickly climbed down and opened the door. "I don't stint on the luxuries."

No, he sure didn't. The interior was leather, the seats cushioned. There was a small bar with liquor bottles and fans in a holder for the ladies and even newspapers to read.

Just then two women came up. Their dresses made Cassie

Pulanski's seem like rags in comparison. Each had a feather in her hat and was twirling a parasol.

"Ransom," said the shapeliest in a sultry purr. "We're looking forward to the entertainment, as always. And we just heard that you have something special cooked up but no one knows what it is."

"All in good time, my dear," Trayburn said. "You have to be patient."

"We're female," the other woman teased. "We don't have a patient bonc in our bodies."

They laughed and swayed off.

"The Jasmine sisters," Trayburn said. "Their family is one of the wealthiest in the territory."

"Must be nice," Fargo said.

Trayburn shrugged. "Their grandfather made the money in shipping and they sit on it. Me, I like to spend mine. To live in style. What good is being rich if you can't enjoy it?"

"I wouldn't know," Fargo said. "I've never been."

"What would you do if you *were* rich? Would you give up being a scout and live like these people do?"

Fargo thought the question was silly but he answered honestly. "I doubt it. I like wandering too much. Not that it will ever happen."

"You never know," Trayburn said.

At eight thirty their little caravan got under way.

The delay was caused by a portly man who showed up late.

"Collander Franks," Trayburn mentioned to Fargo as if he should know the name. "He comes to all my races and bets more than half of the rest combined."

It was quite a procession. Six gun hands rode in front and six more behind. The carriages were resplendent in their finery, the drivers in uniforms like the doorman's.

Ransom Trayburn was astride a handsome bay, his saddle was the best his money could buy. He rode tall and proud, like a king on parade. And he insisted that Fargo ride at his side.

Fargo didn't mind. Trayburn wasn't a gabber. He didn't like having Kiley Strake behind him but Strake didn't strike him as a back shooter.

Only once during the first hour did Trayburn have anything to say, and that was, "I've been meaning to ask. Have you ever taken part in a race? I know you were in a shooting competition once, in Missouri I think it was, against some of the best shooters in the country."

"Damned newspapers," Fargo said.

"You can't hardly blame them," Trayburn said. "It was quite an event. Drew half the state to see it, as I recall."

"Did you read the part where I'm twenty feet tall and breathe fire?"

Trayburn grinned. "It's obvious you're a sporting man. Make me happy and tell me you've raced."

"Once or twice," Fargo said. "But why happy?"

"You'll appreciate my own race that much more," Trayburn said.

"I don't aim to stick around to see it," Fargo informed him. Once he got the Ovaro, he was lighting a shuck for the mountains.

"You never know," Trayburn remarked.

"I do," Fargo said.

At the two-hour mark Trayburn called a halt so his guests could climb out and stretch their legs. The ground had been sloping steadily, if gradually, downward since they left the mile-high city and they were in open prairie with grass and mesquite.

"Aren't you worried they'll figure out where your ranch is?" Fargo asked.

"Look around you," Trayburn said. "See any landmarks?"

No, Fargo didn't.

"These are city folk," Trayburn said. "To them, one spot on the prairie is the same as any other. Hell, half of them can't tell east from west or north from south."

"People can be as dumb as tree stumps," Fargo agreed.

Ransom Trayburn gave him that peculiar look again. "Can't they, though?"

26

About four hours out of Denver the prairie came to an end and ahead stretched dry country broken by sandstone buttes.

Fargo had crossed it a few times in his travels, and in the heat of summer it was hell. It was an unusual place for a ranch.

Trayburn called another halt and everyone climbed out.

They were in jovial spirits, and joked and laughed.

Fargo reined to one side to be by himself. Dismounting, he arched his back and stretched, and smelled perfume.

"Aren't you a handsome devil?" one of the Jasmine sisters said.

"Hope you don't mind that we sought you out," the other offered.

Fargo turned. "Ladies."

"We wanted to look you over," the shapelier of the two said.

"Up close," her younger sister chirped. "To take your measure."

"What did you have in mind?" Fargo said. Not that he would indulge. He was focused on the Ovaro and nothing else.

"Oh, it's not what *we* have in mind," the youngest said, and giggled.

"It's how well you'll do," the shapelier one informed him.

Fargo was about to tell them thanks but no, thanks when a shadow fell across the women and Ransom Trayburn placed a big hand on each of their shoulders. "Girls, girls," he said. "I don't want you bothering this man."

"We were talking to Collander and he told us what you confided in him," the shapeliest said sweetly.

A change came over Ransom Trayburn. He went from friendly to flinty in the bat of an eye. "Didn't you hear me, Gladys?"

Fargo almost laughed at how scared they looked. Gladys apologized and they scooted off.

"Some people just don't listen," Trayburn said, more to himself than to Fargo.

"I didn't mind."

"I don't like being disobeyed. When I say no one is to talk to you, I damn well mean it."

The glimpse of the true Trayburn put Fargo on his guard. But nothing changed. Trayburn continued to be friendly, and the gun hands acted as meek as sheep.

The next hours were spent winding amid a maze of buttes and slashes in the earth made as if by a berserk Almighty with a giant saber.

Those in the windowless carriages couldn't see but Fargo could that they followed a rutted track traveled many times.

He began to think of the bleak landscape as an ocean of arid, which turned out to be fitting when they came on an island of green. A big island some five miles square watered by a stream that came up out of the ground from God-knew-where and flowed to the east to end God-knew-the-same.

The ranch was like everything else Ransom Trayburn owned: grand. In addition to the main house there was a long low building a lot like a bunkhouse for his guests and another long low building that was a bunkhouse for his gun hands. Only in the first they had individual rooms with all the comforts and in the second it was bunks as usual and precious few conveniences.

Fargo was more interested in the stable. As white as a church and almost as high, all it needed was a steeple. It was three times as long as any stable he'd ever seen and lined with stalls from end to end.

Trayburn escorted him inside and over to the third stall on the right. "I believe this is a friend of yours."

Fargo couldn't remember the last time he was choked up. But when the Ovaro nuzzled him and he put his cheek to its neck, he had a lump in his throat and for a minute he couldn't speak. Finally he got out, "Big fella."

The Ovaro nickered.

Fargo entered the stall and examined him from nose to tail. There were no wounds, no bruises, no marks of any kind. He raised a front leg and discovered a new shoe.

"My doing," Trayburn said when Fargo mentioned it. "I told you that I take good care of my horses."

"My horse," Fargo said.

"Yes," Trayburn said, and leaned on his cane. "We need to talk about that."

Fargo stepped in front of the Ovaro with his right hand at his side, brushing his holster. "What are you trying to pull? I thought we had that all settled in Denver?"

"Well, you see," Trayburn said, "I'm afraid it's not as settled as I led you to believe." He pointed his cane to either side.

Down the aisle on the right were three men with rifles trained and on the left were three more. Kiley Strake and Red had followed their boss in and now Red drew his hardware.

"If this isn't enough," Trayburn said, "my men outside have orders to stop you if by some miracle you make it out."

"You son of a bitch."

"That I am," Trayburn said, "and proud of it." He held out his hand. "I'll have your Colt."

"Like hell you will."

"You're quick enough that you might think you can make it. Shoot two or three and duck into the stall and maybe get the rest. But it's not just you, is it? Or didn't you notice where they're pointing those rifles?"

Puzzled, Fargo looked, and his blood ran cold. The riflemen weren't aiming at him. They were aiming at the Ovaro. "I take it back. You're not a son of a bitch. You're a miserable rotten bastard."

"And proud of that, too." Trayburn laughed and crooked his fingers. "The six-gun, if you please."

It went against everything Fargo was and would ever be but he slowly slid his Colt out and handed it over. "So you kill me and keep the Ovaro for yourself?"

"Hell, no," Trayburn said. "What do you take me for?"

"I just told you."

"You don't realize how important you are to me," Trayburn said. "I'll tell you all about it over supper."

"And if I won't go with you?"

"You will, for good reason." Trayburn tossed the Colt to Kiley Strake and stepped to the Ovaro and reached up to pat it but the stallion drew back. "Smart horse."

"Get to the point."

"Fair enough." Trayburn said. "From here on out, you're to do exactly as I say or your horse here dies. You attack anyone, the Ovaro dies. You hit anyone, the Ovaro dies. You try to escape, the Ovaro dies." He indicated the riflemen. "They're not to leave the stable. They'll eat here and sleep here and take turns being ready to put slugs into him if I give them the word or you try to break him out."

"You're holding my horse hostage?"

"That's one way of putting it," Trayburn said. "I like to think of it as insurance that you'll behave until the time comes."

"The time for what?"

"Why, the race of course." Trayburn moved toward the entrance but stopped and looked back. "Let's go. And remember. Be on your best behavior around my guests or you know what will happen." He pointed his finger at the Ovaro and let down his thumb as if it were a trigger and said, "Bang."

Kiley Strake and Red grinned.

Fargo glanced at the Ovaro and said nothing.

"By the way," Trayburn said, "how does it feel to be a tree stump?" And he laughed.

27

It was a wonder Fargo didn't explode. Few times in his life had his blood boiled as it was boiling now. He was beyond angry. Beyond fury. A seething rage gripped him, a rage so overpowering, he saw everything around him as if in a red haze.

He was taken to the ranch house and installed in a bedroom on the second floor and told he was to remain there until Trayburn sent for him.

To ensure he did, three gun hands were in the hall and two more were below his bedroom window.

Fargo paced like a caged tiger. He kept telling himself he should have known. That he was a jackass for ever thinking Ransom Trayburn was a man of his word.

Trayburn had refused to say what he was up to. Later, the big man had said with one of his mocking smiles.

So Fargo fumed and paced. The time passed much more quickly that he would have imagined. The sun was a red bowl of fire on the western horizon when there was a light knock at his door and a female giggled.

Fargo yanked the door open so violently, it was a wonder he didn't rip it from its hinges.

"My word," Gladys Jasmine exclaimed, taking a step back. "You're not about to attack us, are you?"

Her sister giggled.

"What the hell do you two want?" Fargo demanded.

Gladys turned pink and pursed her lips. "Now, now. Be nice. Ransom sent us to fetch you."

"To supper," the other said. "Everyone will be there."

"He thought you might like our company," Gladys said.

Fargo doubted that was the real reason. More likely, Trayburn reckoned he wouldn't attack females.

Gladys held out her arm. She was dressed as if she were going to the theater, with a glittering necklace and a dress that crinkled when she moved. "Shall we?"

Fargo glanced at the guards. All three had their hands on their revolvers. "Why not?" he said. He took her arm and the sister held hers out so he took hers, too.

"These races are always so much fun," Gladys said. "We haven't missed one since they started."

"We love to wager," the nameless sister said. "We win money now and then but we mainly come for the excitement."

"Do you ever gamble?" Gladys asked him.

"I gambled just coming here," Fargo said.

The dining room was as grand as everything else. The guests were seated at a long mahogany table with gleaming silverware and folded napkins. Servants stood ready to wait on their every need.

The sisters brought Fargo to a chair near the head of the table. A servant pulled it out for him and Fargo sat, aware that he was being scrutinized by everyone in the room. They could all go to hell and take Ransom Trayburn with them.

Think of the devil, and he appeared.

Flanked by Kiley Strake and Red, Trayburn sauntered in. He grinned at Fargo, then picked up a spoon and tinkled it against a glass. "Ladies and gents, if you please," he said to silence their chatter. "Permit me to welcome you to the twenty-first Death Race, as I like to call them."

Fargo would never have guessed there had been so many. "You don't call them the Grand Race?"

Trayburn ignored him. To the others he said, "Let's eat, drink and be merry, as they say. At the end of the meal I have a special announcement to make."

"You're fixing to shoot yourself and save me the trouble?" Fargo said.

"I didn't take you for petty," was Trayburn's reply.

"I took you for shit," Fargo said, and this time his thrust succeeded.

Ransom Trayburn colored and his jaw muscles twitched.

"It's not in your best interests to make me mad. If not for your sake, then for the Ovaro's."

"You should kill me while you have the chance," Fargo said. "Because if you don't, I will sure as hell kill you."

"Bluff and bluster don't impress me. I have a small army. You have—what was that word you just used? Oh, yes. You have shit. So spare me your juvenile taunts."

Fargo thought of the Arkansas toothpick in his ankle sheath. But Kiley Strake and Red were watching like a pair of hawks and other bodyguards were nearby.

"Nothing to say? Has some sense trickled into that dense skull of yours? Good." Trayburn gestured imperiously at a waiter. "Start the meal."

They could have called it the Grand Meal. There was beef, there was buffalo, there was venison, there was ham and a turkey. There was a bull's heart, which Fargo rarely saw, stuffed, no less. There were baked potatoes and baked sweet potatoes and mashed potatoes. There was apple butter and regular butter. There were vegetables galore. There was tea and coffee to wash it all down.

The Jasmine sisters preferred to drink bimbos. Made from sugar and brandy with a dash of lemon, the bimbo was popular with those who didn't have to sweat for a living.

Fargo refused to take part. His stomach growled and he mentally told it to shut up.

"You're not eating?" Trayburn asked, a fork of buff meat halfway to his mouth.

Fargo stared.

"Be sensible, for God's sake," Trayburn said. "You need to keep your strength up. Trust me."

"Never again," Fargo said.

Trayburn sighed. "Fine. I savvy that you hate my guts. But you really do need to be at your best, if not for your sake—"

"Let me guess," Fargo interrupted. "For the Ovaro's."

Trayburn nodded.

"What kind of man," Fargo said, "holds a horse over another man's head?"

"The kind who always gets what he wants," Trayburn responded, and laughed.

Reluctantly, Fargo filled his plate and ate. The food was delicious but he refused to savor it.

"Isn't this wonderful?" Gladys asked at one point. "Ransom always has the most heavenly dishes."

"Do you know he once had pheasant?" the other sister said as if pheasant was the Holy Grail of food. "I can't imagine where he got it."

"Probably pulled it out of his ass," Fargo said.

They laughed heartily.

Trayburn said, "I heard that, you son of a bitch."

"I didn't take you for petty," Fargo returned his insult from before.

Trayburn's eyes danced with fire. He suddenly set down his fork and stood. "Ladies and gentlemen," he addressed his guests, "I was going to wait until the meal was over to make an announcement that a few of you know already." He glanced at the Jasmine sisters. "This Death Race is special. One of the riders is a man you might have heard of. A famous scout who will put his life at hazard, the same as the rest of the riders." Trayburn pointed and grinned sadistically. "I give you the famous Skye Fargo."

28

To Fargo's amazement some of the guests clapped.

Gladys nudged him with her elbow and said, "You brave man, you. I wouldn't last half a minute."

"I can hardly ride at all," her sister said.

Trayburn continued. "This Death Race is special in another regard. As many of you know, I likc to liven them up with special challenges. We've had bears. We've had wolves. We've had Crow warriors. Once I had hundreds of rattlesnakes collected and strewn along the racecourse. I spare no expense."

"That you don't, Ransom," Collander Franks spoke up, "and we appreciate your efforts. There is nothing like your races anywhere on earth."

"Why, thank you, Collander," Trayburn said, trying to sound humble. "For this race I've outdone myself. I think you'll agree when you hear the other special surprise I have in store. This year we have"—he paused for effect—"Apaches."

"How in the world?" someone blurted.

"They live a thousand miles south of here," another said.

"Not quite that far," Trayburn replied. "As to the how, I sent a man to Santa Fe and he made the rounds of the forts and was put in touch with a half-friendly Mescalero the whites call Sidewinder. One thing lcd to another, and, well . . ." Trayburn made a movement toward Kiley Strake, who stepped to a door on the left wall and opened it and said something.

Fargo was as dumbfounded as everyone else when four Apaches stalked in. Real, true Apaches, not half bloods. He should know. He'd lived with them.

"I give you Sidewinder and his friends," Trayburn announced with a flourish. "In exchange for new rifles and new knives and horses, they've agreed to take part."

"Good Lord," Gladys said. "The riders have to make it past Apaches to reach the finish line?"

"By God, you've outdone yourself," Collander Franks said, and raised his glass of rum in tribute. "A toast, everyone, to our host."

Fargo was studying the Mescaleros. Stocky and sturdy, wearing breach clouts and knee-high moccasins, they might as well have been carved from stone for all the emotion they showed.

"To make it fair," Trayburn said, "and since the riders are always unarmed, Sidewinder and his friends won't be allowed to use rifles or pistols or even bows and arrows. All they will have are their knives and their wits."

"That should be more than enough," someone said. "Apaches are natural-born killers."

As Fargo well knew. He'd tangled with them more times than he cared to recollect. They were fierce and formidable and deadly as hell.

"This race will be extra exciting," Gladys said giddily.

"I can hardly wait," her sister said.

Fargo would as soon chuck them both off a cliff. He waited until Kiley Strake had ushered the Apaches out and Trayburn had sat back down to say, "If I don't ride in your damn race, I suppose you'll have the Ovaro shot."

"You catch on slow but you catch on," Trayburn said, spearing a piece of buffalo.

"When is it?"

"Tomorrow, unless it rains. The Death Race always starts at noon. They're usually over by one. It's only a mile but the obstacles slow things."

"What others this time besides the Apaches?" Fargo thought he should find out.

"This time, none. I'll go over the rules with you after a while."

"Rules?"

"To make the race fair. If the riders didn't think they stood a chance of winning, no one would take part. You'll meet the others as soon as the meal is done."

"How many?"

"There are always ten, so nine plus you."

Fargo drummed his fingers. So far everything matched with what Phoebe had told him. "Are you holding their horses hostage, too?"

"No need. The winner receives ten thousand dollars. That's more than most of them would see in their lifetime. They'll do whatever they have to in order to win."

"I'd like to hear about those rules now instead of later."

Trayburn set down his fork and ticked them off on his fingers. "The race begins when the starter gun is fired. Any rider who jumps the gun will be shot from their saddle. No weapons are allowed. It's just the rider and his horse. Anyone seen using a weapon will be shot from their saddle. No—"

"Hold on," Fargo said. "Who does all this shooting?"

"Men I post," Trayburn said. "Good shots, every one. Now where was I?" He resumed ticking his fingers. "No dismounting or you'll be shot. No striking another rider with your fists or you'll be shot, but you can do just about anything else to them." He sipped some water. "I had to add that rule for the second race. In the first Death Race, a man got off his horse and hid and beaned some of the other riders with rocks as they rode past him. I call that poor sportsmanship."

"Says the pot to the kettle."

"Insult me all you want," Trayburn said. "It rolls off me like water off a duck." He resumed his recital. "No stopping unless you're forced to or you'll be shot. No food or drink allowed. Smuggle any in and you'll be shot."

"Are we shot if we take a piss?"

"You won't have time for bodily functions. Believe me."

"Does your mother know she raised a son of a bitch?"

"Have your fun. By this time tomorrow you could well be dead." Trayburn smiled. "Or could win. Not just the ten thousand but something that means more to you than I'd ever have guessed." Trayburn chuckled. "All that stuff I fed you about caring for horses and only buying the best because I take pride in good horseflesh?" He shook his head. "I couldn't care less. I buy the best horses because they put on the best races. It's that simple. It's why I bought your Ovaro. Little did I realize it would give me someone to ride him. Someone so stupid, he believed I was sincere."

Fargo came out of his chair so fast, he was on Trayburn before Strake or Red could blink. He slammed a fist into Trayburn's mouth and Trayburn and his chair tipped and crashed over.

Spilling off it, Trayburn levered to his hands and knees. He went to say something, and Fargo drove his boot into his ribs.

The Jasmine sisters screamed. A few men shouted.

Red rushed toward Fargo, drawing his six-shooter. He didn't quite have it out when Fargo caught him with an uppercut that damn near broke his neck.

Hands clutched at Fargo's legs. It was Trayburn, his bloody teeth bared like an animal's. Fargo tried to kick free, stumbled, and wound up on his hands and knees.

Trayburn lunged, and fingers were around his throat. He buried his knuckles in Trayburn's gut but it had no effect so he gouged his thumb at Trayburn's eye.

"What are you waiting for?" Gladys shrieked at someone. "Help Ransom before it's too late!"

Fargo got his hands on Trayburn's throat and they grappled. A knee caught him in the ribs and he butted Trayburn in the face and felt wet drops on his own.

Someone was dancing about at the periphery of Fargo's vision. He didn't dare look but he thought it must be Kiley Strake. He was right. He heard Strake say, "Got you now."

It seemed as if the weight of the world crashed down on Fargo's head.

29

Pain brought Fargo around. Pounding waves of it that made it hard to think. He heard someone groan as if from far away but it was him. He cracked his eyelids and saw a ceiling he didn't recognize, then a face he didn't recognize, either.

"He's comin' around," the face said. It was round and young and topped by a straw hat, of all things. Under the face were bib overalls with suspenders.

"What the hell?" Fargo croaked.

"Howdy, mister," the face said. "I'm Charlie, from Missouri. I reckon you must be a rider like the rest of us or they wouldn't have tossed you in here."

Fargo blinked and stiffly looked around.

Bunks were lined up in two rows the length of a long room. Several men were seated on the bunks they were using.

Others had converged on the one he lay on.

"So this is the great scout?" said a small man in a well-worn suit and a derby.

"He's who, Theo?" Charlie said.

"Weren't you listening, farm boy?" Theo said. "Trayburn added him at the last minute. Seems to think he's something special."

"Go to hell," Fargo rasped. His throat was desert dry. He had to try twice to swallow.

"I'm just saying what we heard," Theo said. "Nothing personal."

"You must have a hard head, mister," Charlie said. "They told us you got clubbed with a gun barrel."

Courtesy of Kiley Strake, Fargo remembered. "This is the bunkhouse for the riders?"

Charlie nodded. "Yep. I've been here over a week. Theo,

that dapper fellow, is from New Orleans. He's been here a little longer."

"And loving every minute," Theo said drily. He held out his hand. "Theodore Tarkis is the name. I'm a jockey. Or I was until the booze ruined me."

Fargo looked at others. None appeared friendly but they weren't unfriendly, either. "You could all die in this race. You know that, don't you?"

"Hellfire, mister," Charlie said with a grin. "For a chance to win ten thousand dollars, I don't care if they can kill me six ways from Sunday."

"That's right," Theo said. "I like the high life and there's been precious little of it for too long."

"Maybe you didn't hear," Fargo said. "This time you're up against Apaches."

"Shucks," Charlie said. "They're just Injuns."

"I'll match my riding against anyone any day of the week," Theo said.

Fargo slowly eased up so his head was propped against a pillow. His hat was on the bunk beside him. "How long have I been out?"

"Half an hour," Charlie said. "I was goin' to slap you to bring you around but Theo said to let you do it on your own."

An older man with near-white hair said, "I'm Buster Langston. The name won't mean anything to you but I used to race in county fairs in Pennsylvania and Ohio."

"How did you find out about the Death Race?" Fargo was curious to learn.

"The same way as most of these others," Buster said. "Trayburn sends people all over to find riders and ask them if they're interested."

"I sure was," Charlie said.

"I understand why the rest of us are here," Buster said. "We want the money. There's not a man among us who wouldn't sell his soul for the ten thousand. But I don't get why a man like you is involved. The way they beat on you, you're not here because you want to be. Am I right?"

Fargo saw no reason not to tell them. "Trayburn has my horse. Unless I take part, he'll shoot it."

"I'll be damned," Buster said.

"I hate anyone who abuses horses," Theo said. "I made my livelihood on them for pretty near twenty years. They're more decent than most people I know."

"My mare, Mabel, is a peach," Charlie said. "I've had her for goin' on five years now."

"Wait," Fargo said. "You brought your own horse to ride?"

"Sure," Charlie said. "So did some of the others. That's allowed. The rest have to pick from the pool."

Several introduced themselves. There was Conklin, from Kentucky. Janks, from Florida. Another man was from Illinois. The only thing they had in common was that they could ride better than most people.

"I can't wait to win," Charlie said. "My ma will be plumb tickled."

"How tickled will she be if you're dead?" Fargo said.

"Hey now," Charlie said, sounding hurt. "No need for talk like that. Mabel will see me through. She always has."

Fargo looked at them and realized there was something else they had in common. They were either down on their luck or past their prime. To them, the ten thousand was a godsend. A new chance at life. It probably hadn't taken much persuasion on Trayburn's part to get them to put their lives at risk. "Have any of you seen where the race is to be held?"

"All of us," Charlie said.

"They took us out there yesterday," Theo informed him.

"To familiarize ourselves, was how Trayburn put it," Buster mentioned.

"What can you tell me?" Fargo asked.

Theo answered with, "It's a canyon. We start at one end and finish at the other. It's fairly straight, no sharp bends and twists. Has to be so the folks who come to watch can see everything."

Charlie nodded. "And it's got cliffs on both sides. We'll be ridin' in the shade."

"How high?" Fargo asked.

"How high what?" Charlie said.

"How high are the goddamned cliffs?"

"Oh. Shucks. I don't know."

"About fifty feet, on average," Buster said.

"That's all?"

"You can't climb them, mister, if that's what you're thinkin'," Charlie said. "They're solid rock and they go straight up."

"Is the canyon narrow or wide?"

"A little of both," Theo said. "It starts out wide but narrows at the middle."

"That's where the boulders are the worst," Charlie said. "We'll have to be careful not to ride into them."

"The Apaches will be right at home," Fargo observed.

"You sure do fret about the redskins," Charlie said. "I fought an Injun boy once and he wasn't hardly nothin'. A Creek, I think he was. He used to hang around the general store and drink a lot. One time he said somethin' to my sis and I laid into him."

Fargo could have told him that comparing a drunk Creek to an Apache was like comparing a house cat to a mountain lion, but what good would it do? He settled for, "You're in over your head, boy."

"I'm a man," Charlie said. "And I'll thank you to stop bein' mean."

"He's actually being nice," Buster said. "He's trying to warn you but you won't listen."

"Warn me about what?"

"The boy is hopeless," Theo said to Fargo. "He can't even get it through his head that he shouldn't be so nice to everyone."

"Why not?" Charlie said. "We're ridin' together, ain't we?"

"Once the race starts, Charlie, it's every rider for himself," Theo said, not unkindly.

"I wish you weren't here, son," Buster said. "I truly do."

Charlie turned to Fargo. "Why is everybody makin' such a fuss over me?"

"Because you're dumb as shit," Fargo said.

"I may not be the best thinker in the world," Charlie said indignantly, "but Ma always said I've got a good heart, and that counts for more."

"Your mother was right, Charlie," Buster said. "But this is no place for a man with a good heart."

"Hell," Fargo said, and swung his legs over the side. He

was about to get up and have a look around when a door at the far end opened.

In strode Ransom Trayburn with Kiley Strake and Red and half a dozen of his gunnies.

"Uh-oh," Charlie said. "Mr. Trayburn looks mad. I wonder who he's mad at."

"That would be me," Fargo said.

30

The riders backed away from Fargo's bunk except for Charlie, who beamed at Ransom Trayburn and said, "Howdy, Mr. Trayburn. I'm sure lookin' forward to tomorrow. Thank you again for the chance to win all that money."

"Shut the hell up, you simpleton," Trayburn snapped. He flicked a finger and Kiley Strake and Red took hold of Charlie's arms and moved him back with the rest.

"Hey," Charlie protested. "What's this?"

Trayburn glared at Fargo. His face was black-and-blue and bruised and swollen, and the eye Fargo had gouged was half shut. "Look at what you did to me."

"It's not nearly enough," Fargo said.

"I should have had you shot. Or better yet, give you to Sidewinder and his friends."

"I'm surprised to still be breathing," Fargo admitted. "Or did you take it out on my horse?"

"Your Ovaro is fine," Trayburn said. "I can't have anything happen to it or you, you bastard. You must have guessed as much or you wouldn't have attacked me."

"You give me too much credit."

"You're the favorite, damn you," Trayburn said.

"Gladys did seem fond of me."

"Not that stupid bitch. The race. You're the odds-on favorite to win. All the big spenders have put their money on you. If you and your horse don't take part, they can withdraw their bets. That's the rule."

"And you do love your rules."

Trayburn bent so they were almost nose to busted nose.

"Just so you know. Even if you do win, this isn't over. It's personal now."

"It always was."

Straightening, Trayburn said, "I've promised you to Kiley. He's lightning in a bottle."

"Never do anything yourself, do you?"

Trayburn ignored the taunt. "I doubt Kiley will get the chance. I had a talk with Sidewinder. I offered ten horses and six rifles to whichever one of them sticks his knife in you."

"We could settle this right now," Fargo said. "The two of us."

"I'm not childish," Trayburn said, drawing himself up to his full height, "and you can't think I'm that stupid."

"Keeping my horse," Fargo said, "was as stupid as it gets."

"Enough of your bluster." Trayburn swiveled on a bootheel and stalked away, Red and the rest falling in behind him.

Kiley Strake lingered. "Between you and me, I hope those red scum don't bury you."

"Brotherly love?"

Strake snorted. "I like to test my mettle against the best. It's been a long time since anyone was half their rep."

"What's that saying?" Fargo said, and pretended to think. "Now I recollect it." He smiled. "Be careful what you wish for."

"You have more sand than a desert," Strake said. "I admire that."

"I'll admire you when the maggots are eating your innards."

Kiley Strake laughed and strolled out.

The moment the door closed, the other riders came to the foot of the bunk.

"God Almighty, mister," Charlie exclaimed. "You've got everybody in creation out to kill you."

"I'm right popular." Fargo rose and rubbed his left shoulder where it was sore from his fight with Trayburn.

"Apaches *and* Kiley Strake *and* Ransom Trayburn," Buster said. "You don't do things by half."

"Don't forget us," Theo the jockey said.

"Us?" Charlie said.

"Are you forgetting the ten thousand?" Theo said. "I'm not letting him or anyone else keep me from winning it. That includes you, boy. Once the race begins, it's every man for himself. I'll ride him down like I would any of you."

"That's not very nice," Charlie said.

"Nice is for simpletons," Theo said. "Which is why you should bow out."

"I ain't simple," Charlie said.

"You won't last half a mile," Theo predicted.

"I'm in it to the end."

"Even if the end is yours?"

On that note they drifted apart. Several went outside. Fargo figured that if they could, he could. But when he opened the door and stepped out into the starlit night, he found himself staring at rifle muzzles.

"That's far enough," a tall drink of water said.

"Mr. Trayburn told us you're to stay put unless he says different," another guard declared.

"Back in you go," ordered a third.

Fargo didn't waste his breath arguing.

He didn't like being cooped up. He paced the aisle or stared out the windows. Everyone avoided him as if he had the plague or was bad luck. With one exception.

"Mind if I join you, mister?" Charlie asked.

Fargo was at a window that afforded a view of the stable. "You should have listened to Buster," he said.

"Eh?" Charlie glanced at the old man, who was resting on his bunk. "Oh. That again. I couldn't if I wanted to, which I don't. That money means Ma can live out her days without any worries."

"You're doing this for her?"

"Well, me too. I'll keep half."

"I could try to help you get away."

"No, damn it. Why does everybody treat me like I'm a kid? I'm seein' this through. Worry about yourself. I have God on my side."

"God?"

"I prayed to him like Ma taught me, and I'll let you in on a secret." Charlie stepped closer and lowered his voice. "The reason I ain't worried? God told me I'm goin' to win."

"Jesus, boy," Fargo said.

"No," Charlie replied, and beamed. "It was God. I was prayin' and I heard a voice as clear as anything in my head. It said, 'Charlie, you all are goin' to win.'"

"So that's how God talks."

"Eh? Oh. I reckon God talks to each of us like we'd talk to ourselves."

"If you say so."

"Yes, sir," Charlie said, nodding and smiling. "I'm goin' to win and have all that money and live happily ever after, like in one of them fairy tales Ma used to read to me when I was a sprout."

"Seems to me," Fargo said, "that your head is full of fairy tales."

"It used to be," Charlie said. "There's that one about the tar baby. And the one about the ant and the cricket, I think it was. And my favorite, the bean one."

"Don't forget the one about the boy from Missouri who thinks God told him he's going to win a race."

"That's just mean."

"If you want to see mean," Fargo said, "wait until the race starts and everyone is out to stop you."

"Me and God," Charlie said, "we'll lick 'em."

31

The night dragged like it would take forever.

Fargo tried to sleep but barely managed a wink. He needed the rest to be sharp for the race but every time he drifted off, he woke up with a start within only a few minutes. He was too wrought up.

Finally he lay listening to the snores and mutters of the others until the crow of a cock heralded the day of the Death Race.

At six the riders were allowed to go eat breakfast.

"Not you," a guard snapped when Fargo tried to leave. "The boss says you stay put."

"Someone will bring you your eats soon enough," another informed him.

Someone did—Gladys Jasmine. She acted unsure of how he'd behave and stopped short to say, "I've brought your breakfast."

"I can see it and smell it," Fargo said. The tray had a heaping portion of eggs, bacon and toast, and coffee. If nothing else, Trayburn fed the riders well. His stomach growled.

"You're not mad at me, are you? For yelling for help when you attacked Mr. Trayburn yesterday?"

"You can't help being you."

"I'm happy you're being reasonable. You don't like him much, do you?"

"About as much as I like what comes out his ass."

"Goodness, you can be crude," Gladys said, but she grinned. "Ransom asked me to bring this because he said I was the one person you wouldn't hurt."

"I thought it would be Strake," Fargo told her. "Him and me are pards now."

She set the tray on his bunk and then sat next to the tray. "Mind if we talk?"

"Gab away," Fargo said, and for once in his life, he meant it. He picked up the tray and placed it on his lap.

"You have Ransom so mad, it's almost funny."

"I'll laugh after I eat."

"I'm serious. You jumping him like that, and making a mess of his handsome face. No one has stood up to him in a very long time."

"I aim to do more standing," Fargo said, and treated himself to a spoonful of scrambled eggs.

"He might have had you drawn and quartered, only you're too important to the race. Half the people have bet on you and that fine horse of yours." Gladys wriggled excitedly. "My sister and I put fifteen thousand on you but then Collander Franks wagered fifty thousand and we had to match him."

"You had to?"

"It's the rules," Gladys said. "It's not like at a normal racetrack."

"How does it work?" Not that Fargo cared but it would be nice to know.

"Everyone places their bets. If two people bet on the same rider, they have to bet the same amount. All of it goes into a pot."

"Keep going," Fargo said with his mouth full. "Why the same amount?"

"Because if one person bet ten thousand and the other person bet five thousand, that wouldn't be fair to the person who bet ten, would it, silly goose?" Gladys cheerily grinned. "The money goes into a common pot. Let's say that all together half a million dollars is bet. It's often that high or higher. We take our betting seriously."

"Good for you," Fargo encouraged her.

"So, let's say, in a typical race three or four people bet on the winning rider. They get to divide up the entire pot."

Fargo whistled.

"Yes, it's a very large amount of money," Gladys said. "Which is why these Death Races of Ransom's are so popular." She paused. "That, and they're just so much fun to watch.

132

One year I saw a grizzly tear a rider to pieces. Another time a rattlesnake bit a horse and when it fell it threw its rider and he split his skull on a boulder."

"Sounds like a barrel of fun."

"Oh, you have no idea," Gladys said, and laughed.

Fargo bit a piece of toast. "Do the rest feel like you do?" he asked with his mouth full.

"There are a few who don't like the blood and the dying, I suppose," Gladys said, "but they're wet blankets."

"Imagine not wanting to see folks die."

"Exactly. It's not as if anyone forces the riders to take part." She caught herself. "Well, except for you. Which is why my sister and me are hoping you'll win."

"You're too kind," Fargo said. "Tell me. Are there any kids at this thing?"

"Kids? Heavens, no. Who would bring children to a spectacle like this. It's for adults only. That's another of Ransom's rules."

"There's that word again."

"Rule?"

"Spectacle."

"That's what Ransom calls them, and it fits. The Death Races are like those games the old Romans used to put on. At that Colosseum place in Italy."

"Dying isn't a game if you're one of the ones who might die."

"But it's sure exciting to watch. My sister and I wouldn't miss a Death Race for the world."

"Any chance you could slip me a weapon before the race begins?"

"How can you even ask?" Gladys was shocked. "A rider isn't allowed to have any. It wouldn't be fair to the other riders."

"And we want the races to be fair."

"Yes, we do. Why do you sound so mad? You'll have the same chance as everyone else."

"It doesn't bother you that there will be four Apaches out there trying to kill every rider they can?"

"Goodness, no. That's the best part."

"Ah," Fargo said.

"I don't know as I like your tone. Here Ransom has given you a great honor. Not everybody gets to ride in a Death Race."

"Throw a starving dog a bone and the dog thinks you're doing it a favor."

"You say the strangest things," Gladys said, and shook her head. "Honestly, you confuse me. Instead of being so angry, you should be grateful. Only a few of the riders actually ever die. The winner gets ten thousand, as you must already know, and the losers are paid five hundred each and sent on their way." She wagged a finger. "Think of the money and nothing else and it will see you through."

"I'm thinking of the killing," Fargo said.

32

It was called a Death Race but it had a carnival atmosphere.

The riders were brought out at ten. All the guests had gathered in front of the ranch house and Ransom Trayburn gave a talk about how fine a day it promised to be and everyone should eat, drink and make merry. The guests applauded.

Then Trayburn turned to the riders. "As for you men, I salute you. It takes great courage to do what you're about to do."

"For that much money," Charlie exclaimed, "we'll have courage to spare."

Some of the guests laughed.

Fargo stood by himself at the center of a ring of three guards with leveled rifles. Trayburn was making sure he didn't try anything before the race commenced.

The happy faces of the guests lent fire to Fargo's fury. They were as much to blame for the Death Race as their host. Sure, it was Trayburn who staged them. But if there weren't people like these, people willing to bet on human life, there wouldn't be a Death Race.

Human nature, Fargo had long ago learned, wasn't anything to brag about.

"After the race there will be a banquet to celebrate," Trayburn reminded them, "with music and dancing and a fine time for all."

Charlie whooped for joy.

Fargo looked away in disgust and saw Gladys and her sister. Both waved at him and Gladys blew him a kiss.

"Bitches and sons of bitches," Fargo said under his breath.

It wasn't long before their horses were brought over by stable hands.

Fargo moved to the Ovaro and his guards went with him. He patted and rubbed the stallion's neck and noticed that the saddle was his. The scabbard was empty, though, and his saddlebags were missing.

Open carriages were brought and the guests piled in.

With Ransom Trayburn at the head and the riders close behind flanked by riflemen, the procession headed north to the canyon, which turned out to be less than ten minutes away.

At the canyon mouth the carriages split, with some of the guests bearing along the east rim and the rest along the west.

Fargo and the other riders were held at the starting point.

So far there had been no sign of Sidewinder and the rest of the Apaches. Fargo figured they were already in the canyon, waiting in ambush.

Kiley Strake rode up, with Red along.

"I wish you luck," Strake said.

"Go to hell."

"I mean it," Strake said. "I won't get to try you if you're dead."

"I'm the one who should kill him," Red said. "He hit me."

"He's mine," Strake said. "Don't you forget that."

Fargo smiled. "Girls, girls. There's no need to fight over me."

Red bristled and cursed but Kiley Strake laughed. "Don't pay him any mind, Red. He's trying to get your goat so you'll be easier to kill."

"It's not working," Red snapped.

"Remember you said that," Fargo said, "when I put a slug in you."

The canyon was exactly as it had been described, with cliffs on either side. Canvas pavilions had been set up at the cliff edges so the guests could observe the spectacle in comfort.

The riders had to wait while the carriages carried the guests to their assigned pavilions.

Men with rifles, Fargo noticed, were posted near each one.

Ransom Trayburn rode up astride a magnificent chestnut. "Gentlemen," he said, "the moment of truth is upon you. I'll be on the rim"—he pointed at the east side—"following your progress. Remember the rules. I don't want to have to shoot any of you but I will if you break them."

"Shucks, Mr. Trayburn," Charlie said. "After how nice you've been to us, I'll stick to your rules like they were glue." He beamed proudly.

"I'm sure you will, Charlie," Trayburn said. "It's one or two of these others I'm thinking of." He looked pointedly at Fargo and then at Theo the jockey.

"I won't cheat," Theo said.

"I hope not," Trayburn said. "But you've cheated before, haven't you? That's part of why you couldn't find work. No one likes a man who resorts to dirty tricks."

Fargo laughed.

"I know what you're thinking," Trayburn said, "and I resent it."

"One of us," Fargo said, "doesn't give a good damn what you resent."

Buster, the rider from Pennsylvania, cleared his throat. "Mr. Trayburn, I've got a question about these Apaches of yours."

"Apaches don't belong to anyone," Trayburn said. "But go ahead and ask."

"I don't think you played fair with us," Buster surprised Fargo by saying. "When you talked me into this, you told me about others races when you've had bears and wolves and whatnot. You never said anything about Apaches."

"I told you about the Crows who took part once in return for a case of whiskey. I was clear that hostiles might be part of it."

"Even so," Buster said. "I may be from the East but even I know that Crows ain't Apaches."

"Do you want to back out?"

Buster hesitated, then shook his head. "No, sir. I was only getting it off my chest. But there is something else I'd like to know."

"I'm listening."

"You've gone on about how they'll be out to kill us," Buster said. "Can we kill them if we have to?"

"Of course. What do you take me for? It would hardly be fair if you couldn't."

Charlie said, "You're a fine gent, Mr. Trayburn, sir, and that's for sure."

Fargo sniffed loudly and said, "Anyone else smell that?"

"Smell what?" Charlie said.

Fargo sniffed again. "It smells like the biggest pile of horseshit in all creation."

Ransom Trayburn wasn't amused. "There are limits to how much I'll abide."

"Funny thing," Fargo said. "I'm the same way."

Trayburn raised his reins. "I can't wait for one of the Apaches to carve out your heart." He wheeled the chestnut and barked at Kiley Strake, "Get them lined up. When I give the signal, fire the shot."

"I know what to do, boss," Strake said.

Fargo found himself positioned in the middle, between Theo and Buster. Charlie and his mare, Mabel, were at the far left.

All the riders were focused on Strake. Not Fargo. He was looking at the ground ahead, and what he saw made him grimly smile.

"Get set, gents," Kiley Strake said. He drew his pearl-handled Remington and cocked it.

Trayburn and several gun hands had galloped up to the first pavilion. Trayburn dismounted and consulted his pocket watch. The sun was almost directly overhead.

"Here we go, fellas," Charlie exclaimed.

Trayburn was staring at his watch. Suddenly he raised his left arm and waved

Kiley Strake fired into the air.

The Death Race had begun.

33

The Ovaro exploded into motion at a jab of Fargo's spurs.

From the heights came cheers and whoops and yells but the spectators were quickly drowned out by the thundering hooves of the ten horses.

Fargo glanced back. He'd pulled ahead but not by much. Charlie and his mare and Theo on a bay were second and third. Buster and the rest were bunched up behind them.

He stayed in the lead for another hundred yards. That was far enough, he figured. Without being obvious, he slowed. Not a lot, just enough that within moments Charlie and Theo overtook him. He let them race past and Charlie cackled.

"See you at the finish line!"

Fargo hoped the boy made it. As for him, he wasn't out to win. He was out for blood.

Trayburn thought he had the upper hand because every element of the race was under his control. No weapons allowed for the riders, and the riflemen on the rims, were to ensure that no one tried anything.

But Trayburn had overlooked something important. Something Fargo could use to his advantage.

The canyon walls were too sheer to climb and solid rock, but the canyon floor was ordinary dirt. A racing horse raised a lot of dust. Ten horses raised a god-awful amount. So much, that in the time it took the riders to reach the two-hundred-yard mark, a thick cloud had risen.

The lead riders were spared the worst of it. But not the riders farther back.

Which was why Fargo had slowed. The dust had swallowed him and the Ovaro—and hid them from the watchers on the rims. He kept slowing until he was last, which was exactly where he wanted to be. That was where the dust was thickest.

It caked him and the Ovaro. It got into his eyes and his nose. It made him cough.

Ahead, a horse whinnied and a man screamed.

Fargo had a hunch why. The Apaches. They would have spread out the length of the canyon, and one was bound to have chosen this end.

A boulder loomed. Fargo reined aside and barely missed it, then had to haul on the reins to keep from colliding with a horse that was on the ground, thrashing.

The instant he stopped, a stocky figure hurtled out of the dust. Steely fingers wrapped around his leg. Before he could break free, his boot was wrenched from the stirrup and he was upended.

Fargo came down hard on his shoulders. He rolled over and pushed up into a crouch, darting his hand into his boot as he rose.

Nearby lay a rider gouting blood from a slit throat.

The Apache responsible must have thought he had another easy victim because he came at Fargo with his knife raised high.

Sidestepping, Fargo drove the toothpick to the hilt into the warrior's belly and sliced upward. The flesh parted like a torn water skin and out spilled not water but blood and gore and intestines.

The Apache stiffened and looked down at himself as if he couldn't believe what he was seeing. *"To-dah,"* he said, and went to stab Fargo but he was dead before he could bury his knife.

Fargo yanked the toothpick out, quickly wiped it on one of the Apache's knee-high moccasins, and slid it into its sheath. The warrior's own blade had fallen from his outstretched hand, and Fargo snatched it up and wedged it under his belt.

The Ovaro had stopped when he was pulled off. Grabbing the saddle horn, he swung up and was at a gallop again not sixty seconds after he had been unhorsed.

Fargo braced for shots from above but none came. It was

as he thought—the riflemen couldn't see clearly in the dust soup. They hadn't seen him use the toothpick.

He lashed his reins and the Ovaro became a bolt of four-legged lightning. Ahead appeared vague shapes on horse-back. He glimpsed a tail and the back of a man's head.

Up on the cliffs people were cheering and yelling but as before their words were lost in the din.

A horse and its rider materialized out of the dust. Something was wrong, and the animal was limping.

Fargo shot past, or tried to. The man's arm flicked out and he clutched at Fargo's shirt. His intention was plain. To pull Fargo off and take the Ovaro for himself. Fargo clubbed him with his fist and was in the clear.

Another boulder rose out of nowhere and Fargo reined sharply to avoid it. He did the same with another, and yet a third, and realized they were everywhere, inviting disaster.

A horse squealed stridently and there was the crash of a heavy body.

A few more moments and Fargo was abreast of a sorrel on its side with two broken front legs. It would have to be put out of its misery. Its rider already was; the man had apparently pitched headfirst into the boulder that brought the horse down and the impact had crushed his skull as if it were a melon.

Fargo was keeping a tally. Three riders down, seven left, including himself. Three Apaches left, too.

And there one was, partially visible in the dust, bent over a hapless rider, a knife imbedded in the man's throat.

It was Buster, the man from Pennsylvania, wheezing and spraying scarlet.

The Apache whirled toward the Ovaro.

Fargo rode him down. He jabbed his spurs and the stallion slammed into the warrior at a full gallop.

Over a thousand pounds of muscle and heavy bone moving at over thirty miles an hour hit the Apache like a battering ram.

Fargo swept on by and looked over his shoulder. A crumpled, broken, bloody heap was all that was left of Apache Number Two. He patted the Ovaro and smiled.

The boulders stopped appearing. It could be he was in a clear stretch. Hoping that was the case, he rose in the stirrups and scanned both rims. He couldn't see all that well because of the dust but well enough to make out the riders and carriages hurrying off to be in on the finish of the race.

The riflemen were going, too.

Abruptly drawing rein, Fargo held himself and the Ovaro still. If anyone spotted him, he'd be a sitting duck. But the clatter of wheels and vocal racket from above faded, and no one took a shot at him.

He wheeled the stallion. The dust made it hard to be sure but he wasn't more than a fourth of the way into the canyon. If his luck held, he'd reach the starting point well before the winner—and all the spectators—reached the finish line.

Fargo thought of Trayburn, and everything that had been done to him. How Trayburn lied and threatened the Ovaro and mocked him at every turn. And his blood boiled.

Soon he would be out of the canyon, and would find a spot to lie low. Then it was just a matter of waiting for night to fall.

Ransom Trayburn didn't know it yet, but their fight was just starting.

34

Stars twinkled in a clear sky, and a breeze blew from out of the north. Coyotes yipped but otherwise the wildlife was quiet.

The same couldn't be said of the human variety. The ranch house was ablaze with light. Every window glowed, and shadows moved across many of the panes.

The celebration was in full swing. The wafting notes of a violin told Fargo that the meal was over and the dance had begun.

Good, he thought. Let them laugh and play and drink themselves into a stupor.

Trayburn's protectors were another matter. They'd be sober and on their guard.

Fargo circled to approach from the opposite direction from the canyon. He was acting on the assumption that Trayburn knew he'd gotten away and would expect him to want to even the score.

Then again, maybe not. Trayburn might think that he had done what any sensible man would do, namely, lit a shuck while he could.

Some men tucked tail as naturally as breathing. Not Fargo. He never backed down, never turned a cheek, never, ever quit. Some might say it was his pride. Some might say he was being pigheaded.

Fargo saw it different. He saw it as standing up for himself. No one had the right to ride roughshod over others. When that happened, his natural instinct was to feed them their teeth.

He was close enough now that he could see the horses in

the corral at the rear of the stable. Many were dozing. None whinnied as he came to a stop.

Climbing down, he wrapped the reins around a rail. As a precaution he removed his spurs. It wouldn't do to have them jingle at the wrong moment. Since he didn't have his saddlebags he left the the spurs lying next to a post.

His saddlebags. His Henry. His Colt. He aimed to get all three back.

That, and a few gallons of blood, should about make things right.

Climbing over the rails, he crept to the rear door. It was partially open. He took off his hat and peered in.

Up at the front was one of Trayburn's shoot-for-hires.

The man was leaning against a double door, looking as bored as a man could look. He had his back to the center aisle.

Donning his hat, Fargo slipped inside. He hugged the shadows, freezing when the gun hand yawned and again when the man stretched.

Halfway there he was about to palm the Arkansas toothpick when he noticed something leaning against a stall. It would do even better.

Gripping the long handle in both hands, he made it to the last of the stalls without being seen. He had to cross ten feet of open space. If the man heard him and was quick on the shoot, it might as well be a mile.

Fargo coiled, then threw himself forward. The man jerked erect and turned. Shock registered an instant before Fargo drove the pitchfork's tines into his chest.

With a gurgle and a feeble claw for his pistol, the man melted.

Fargo helped himself to a Colt. It wasn't his but it would do. He checked that it was loaded and twirled it to get a feel for how it molded to his hand.

There was a lot more than ten feet of space between the stable and the ranch house. More like a hundred, awash in starlight.

The ranch house would wait, though. He was saving the best for last.

Only one window gleamed in the bunkhouse. Three men

were playing cards at a small table. The rest must be at the house.

Fargo quietly worked the latch. It scraped but not loud enough for them to hear.

They were so intent on their card game that they didn't look up until he was almost to the table. The click of the Colt's hammer caught their attention, and they did what anyone with common sense would do: they froze.

"Gents," Fargo said.

"It's him!" a string bean declared.

"I'll kill any one of you sons of bitches who doesn't do what I say when I say it," Fargo told them. "If you savvy, nod."

Three heads bobbed in unison.

"Good. You're just hired help, so you get to live but not if you make me mad." Fargo pointed at the string bean. "You. Put down your cards and stand."

The man anxiously complied, his hands splayed. Coughing, he said, "What do you aim to do with us, mister?"

"Did I say you could talk?"

"No."

"Then it's pretty goddamn stupid to flap your gums, isn't it?"

The string bean went to reply, thought better of it, and clamped his mouth shut.

"You learn quick," Fargo said, and looked around. "Is there any rope in here?"

The man shook his head.

Fargo spotted a rifle propped against a bunk. "See that Spencer?"

The man looked and nodded.

"Go over and pick it up by the end of the barrel and bring it over. Do it slow or I'll shoot you. You try to grab it by the stock and I'll shoot you. Are you hankering to die?"

The man shook his head.

"Good. Now fetch it."

The other two might as well have been chiseled from stone.

When the man with the Spencer was almost to the table, Fargo told him to stop.

"Stand behind your friend with the checkered shirt."

Looking puzzled, the string bean did as he was told.

"Now hit him over the head hard enough to knock him out."

"What?" the man in the chair said.

Fargo pointed his Colt at the string bean. "I'm waiting, and I won't wait long."

The *thunk* was quite loud. The man in the chair slumped with his cheek on the table and spittle dribbling over his chin.

"Now move behind your other friend."

"Hold on," the other friend said. "Can't you just tie us up?"

"No rope, remember?" Fargo said. "Do it."

The second *thunk* wasn't as loud but the result was the same.

"Now set the rifle on the table and take three steps back and turn around."

"Oh, God," the string bean said.

"You're talking again." Fargo holstered the Colt and wrapped his hands around the barrel.

"Happy to help," the man said, but he didn't sound happy at all.

"Look at the bright side."

"There is one?"

"You get to live," Fargo said. He went to swing, and had a thought. "How many gun hands at the main house?"

"Six."

"You're lying," Fargo said. "There are more of you than that."

"Collander Franks had to get back to Denver right away, so Mr. Trayburn sent four men along to guard him. Four more are over at the woodshed. That's where Mr. Trayburn stuck the redskins."

"Why stuck?" Fargo said.

"Mr. Trayburn aims to kill Sidewinder and that other buck in the morning. They've served their purpose, as he put it."

"So he even lied to them."

"They're just Apaches. Why wouldn't he?"

"Before I forget, who won the damn Death Race?"

"That kid from Missouri, Charlie what's-his-name. You should have heard him whoop and holler."

"Good for him," Fargo said, and swung.

So far it had been unexpectedly easy. But he was under no delusion it would stay that way.

Dropping the Spencer on a bunk, he went back out.

Music and mirth filled the night. Everyone at the ranch house was having a fine time.

"Soon," Fargo said.

35

The woodshed was over by the outhouses. It wasn't much bigger than they were. There were no windows, and a bar across the door.

Two of the four pistols-for-hire were leaning against the shed. The other two had hunkered with their rifles across their laps. They were talking.

Fargo was flat on his belly, snaking silently, when he recognized one of the voices.

". . . have to stay out here watching these damn vermin when we could be inside sneaking drinks and food," Red complained.

"It's your own fault," another replied. "The boss is mad at you on account of that scout."

"He walloped you twice," a third said. "That's mighty careless."

"The first time he caught me by surprise," Red grumbled.

"Any hombre who make his livin' chuckin' lead," declared the fourth, "can't afford surprises."

"Amen, brother," said the second.

"You weren't there. What do you know?" Red took to pacing and glaring at the ranch house. "I get stuck with you while that damn Kiley Strake lives it up."

"Don't let Strake hear you say that. It ain't healthy."

"I'm not afraid of him," Red said.

"You should be."

By then Fargo was close enough. He swept up and slammed the Colt against Red's temple, then trained the Colt on the others before they could so much as breathe.

"Who wants lead in them?"

A man leaning against the shed flung his rifle into the

grass. "Not me, mister. Don't shoot. Trayburn doesn't pay me enough to die for him."

"Me either," a second agreed.

"Toss the rifles and then the sidearms," Fargo commanded, "like a turtle would."

"Just don't shoot us."

Once they were disarmed, Fargo had them move to one side. Covering them, he lifted the bar and said in the Mescalero tongue, "Come out."

Sidewinder warily emerged, the other warrior close behind. They looked at the three with their arms up and at Red on the ground, and at Fargo.

"You talk our tongue?" Sidewinder asked.

"A little," Fargo said, and switched to English. "Do you speak the white man's?"

"A little," the Mescalero said.

"The white-eye who brought you here intends to kill you."

Sidewinder grunted, which was the Apache way of saying he knew.

"My guess is he doesn't want anyone to hear about your part in his Death Race," Fargo said.

"Him say he friend," Sidewinder said. "Him speak with two tongues."

"How would you like to pay him back?"

"What that?" Sidewinder said.

Fargo rephrased it. "How would you and your friends like to kill a lot of whites and help me burn this place to the ground?"

Sidewinder said something in his own tongue to the other warrior, who grunted. "Red Wolf and me like very much." He cocked his head. "But why you do this? Why you help Apache?"

"I have lived with the *Shis-Inday*," Fargo said, using their word for themselves. To be exact, he had lived with an Apache woman, and God, she had been a she-cat under the blankets.

"You friend to Apache?"

"Sometimes," Fargo said. Although, the truth be known, he'd fought them more times than he befriended them. "The

150

important thing is that right here and now, your enemy is my enemy."

Sidewinder made a sound remarkably like, "Ah."

"Kill as many whites as you want," Fargo said. "Take as many of their horses as you want. Except for the Ovaro at the corral. He's mine. Take him and I will hunt you down."

"What you do while we kill whites?"

"I'll be killing them too," Fargo said. He stepped to a rifle and tossed it to Sidewinder, who deftly caught it. "Start whenever you want. But we want to do it quiet at first so those in the house don't hear us and head for the hills."

"Quiet," Sidewinder said. His right hand dipped to his knee-high moccasin and rose holding a long knife. Before anyone could guess his intent, he'd bent and slashed Red's throat.

"Oh, God," one of the other men blurted, and the three turned to run off.

The Apaches were on them like quicksilver ghosts. Sidewinder's knife flashed and Red Wolf used his hands, and it was over.

"Help yourself to any weapons you want," Fargo said, and made for the house. Midway there he acquired two shadows.

A leather-slapper was on the front porch, his shoulder to a post. He was alert and tapping his boot to the music. There was no way to get to him without him seeing.

Fargo looped to the back of the house. There were two doors. He chose the nearest, and cracked it open.

The Apaches stood back, eyeing him like cats. They didn't fully trust him but they were going along with him for the time being. Which suited him fine.

A large kitchen was being cleaned by several cooks and their helpers. Some were women and bound to scream at sight of the Apaches.

Fargo closed the door and moved to the next. It opened into an empty hall. He slipped in, the Apaches padding like wraiths after him.

The music and hubbub of voices grew louder.

At a junction Fargo halted. He heard a feminine laugh and poked his head out.

Two women and a man were strolling toward an open

door at the other end. Fargo could see dancers, and beyond them, musicians.

The threesome were merrily chatting but stopped when someone else came ambling out.

Young Charlie was so drunk he swayed like a sailor on a storm-tossed deck. "Ladies!" he happily declared. "How would you like to dance with the winner of the race?"

The fancy women in their perfect dresses drew back as if afraid he would touch them. The man they were with puffed out his chest and said, "Here now, boy. Behave yourself."

"All I did was ask," Charlie said, and walked by them, winking and grinning at the ladies.

The trio hustled to the main room and went in.

Charlie lurched against a wall, bounced off, and lurched against the other wall. "How in hell do I get to the outhouse?" he asked himself.

Fargo waited. In a few more steps the boy would reach them.

That was when, without warning, Sidewinder sprang past him with his knife poised to stab.

36

Fargo acted without thinking and grabbed the Apache's wrist. Quick as thought, Sidewinder turned on him and tried to wrest loose. *"To-dah,"* Fargo said in their tongue, which meant no. "He is a friend."

Sidewinder looked at Charlie in contempt and said, *"Tagoon-ya-dah,"* or, "He is a fool."

Charlie stood with his mouth agape, his breath a distillery in itself. "Fargo? Is that you?"

Letting go of Sidewinder, Fargo grabbed Charlie by the shirt and hauled him around the corner before someone at the dance spotted them. He pressed him to the wall and put a hand over his mouth. "Keep it down, you hear?"

Charlie nodded. When Fargo removed his hand, Charlie grinned. "I'm right happy to see you. Mr. Trayburn won't be, though. He's got some of his men out hunting for you."

"Where's Mabel?"

"My sweetheart of a mare? She's over to the stable. I fed her oats as a treat for winning." Charlie giggled. "I'm rich, by God."

"Did Trayburn give you your winnings yet?"

Charlie nodded. "In my saddlebags in my room."

"Fetch them and get Mabel and head for Missouri and your ma," Fargo said. "It's about to get ugly."

Only then did Charlie seem to belatedly realize the two Apaches were there. He blinked and said, "I must be seeing things. You're with the redskins now?"

"You need to go," Fargo said. He couldn't afford the delay. Any moment, someone might discover the dead men at the woodshed or the men in the bunkhouse and give the alarm.

"What are you fixin' to do?" Charlie asked. "I hope you're not out to hurt anybody. These are awful nice folks."

"Like hell." Fargo gave the boy a slight push. "Off you go."

Charlie took a step but stopped. "I don't like bein' shoved. And I don't like redskins."

"Damn it, boy."

"And I don't like bein' cussed at. I'm a growed man, not no boy. I don't know what you're up to but it can't be good and I'm goin' to let everyone know." Charlie opened his mouth to shout.

Sidewinder slipped a hand past Fargo and stabbed Charlie in the heart.

Charlie looked down at himself, said, "That wasn't nice," and collapsed.

Fargo swore. He reminded himself he needed the Apaches, if only for a while yet. Opening a door, he dragged Charlie in and was going back out when he realized he was in a library or study with books on three walls and a desk in the center. On the desk, like a godsend from heaven, were his Henry and his Colt.

"I'll be damned." Fargo tossed the six-shooter he'd been using to Sidewinder and scooped up his own. He checked that it was still loaded and twirled it into his holster. The Henry was loaded, too.

The Mescaleros waited expectantly.

"Hunt and kill," Fargo said in their tongue.

"What you do?" Sidewinder asked in English.

Fargo told them.

Sidewinder smiled and said, "You make good Apache." Then they were gone.

Fargo yanked out the drawers. In the second on the left he found a pipe and tobacco, and lucifers. More than enough for his purpose.

The stairs were down a side hall. He barreled into the first room he came to on the second floor. It was a bedroom that smelled of perfume. Female effects were scattered about.

Using the toothpick, Fargo shredded a quilt and cut up a blanket and piled them under a window. He opened it enough for air to get in, squatted, and lit a lucifer. The down in the quilt caught right away. Small flames became large flames that rapidly climbed a curtain.

Fargo raced downstairs. No more skulking. He strode straight for the spacious parlor.

The celebration was at its height, liquor flowing like water. Guests were dancing or seated at tables or standing around talking and flirting and being merry.

Ransom Trayburn was at a table by himself, about to pour a drink. Kiley Strake flanked him and other gun sharks were to either side.

Fargo started with them. He stood in the doorway, jammed the Henry to his shoulder, and shot a bewhiskered killer smack between the eyes. He jacked the lever, shot another in the chest, jacked the lever, shot a third in the face.

It took that long for the guests to wake up to what was happening. Women wailed and men cursed and yelled, and panic spread like a prairie fire.

Fargo swiveled toward the chair with Ransom Trayburn— only Trayburn wasn't there. He was going out the far end, Strake and two gun hands at his back.

Set to go after them, Fargo caught movement out of the corner of his eye. A guest had swept his jacket aside and was unlimbering a pocket pistol. He shot the man in the jaw and saw teeth and bone explode. Another whipped a revolver out and got off a shot that went wide. Fargo drilled him.

By now guests were fleeing for the doors and some were going out windows.

Fargo ran after Trayburn. No one tried to shoot him. He saw the front door was wide open and figured Trayburn had fled.

Just then a gun hand popped out of a doorway and fanned two quick shots.

Fargo dived the instant the shooter appeared and the slugs thwacked the wall above him. In midair he pointed the Henry and squeezed, and scarlet spurted from the man's throat.

Fargo pushed up, vaulted over the thrashing *pistolero*, and sprinted to the front door. In his eagerness to catch up to Trayburn, he blundered. He bounded out onto the porch without looking first.

Straight into a gun muzzle.

37

Surprise saved Fargo's hide. The man hadn't expected him to come barreling out and recoiled and fanned a shot from the hip. The slug struck the jamb.

Fargo only had to thrust the Henry at the man's chest, and squeeze. At the blast his would-be killer staggered to the steps and tumbled.

Ducking in case there were others ready to shoot, Fargo darted to the rail. When no gunfire crashed, he vaulted over. He came down hard on his bootheels and pressed his left hand to the ground to keep from pitching flat.

People were still pouring from the house and running every which way.

Above their cries and shrieks rose Apache war whoops and the boom of guns.

One of Trayburn's protectors spilled around the side of the porch, his smoke wagon in hand. He spotted Fargo and jerked his revolver up.

Fargo cored his brainpan. He worked the lever to feed a fresh cartridge into the Henry's chamber, and happened to glance at the stable.

Ransom Trayburn and some others were just disappearing inside.

Fargo went after them. A loud crackling drew his gaze back to the house.

Flames were leaping from the second-floor window and climbing up the front wall. Already part of the roof was on fire. Unless a bucket brigade was organized, and quickly, the ranch house would burn to the ground.

That suited Fargo just fine. But destroying it wouldn't put

a stop to the Death Races. The only way to do that was to deal with the bastard responsible.

Fargo approached the stable so as not to silhouette himself against the open doors. He was almost there when a spate of shots from the house caused him to stop and crouch. But no one was shooting at him.

Sidewinder and Red Wolf had found rifles somewhere, and burst out spraying lead. Half a dozen guests were felled in their tracks, men and women. The Apaches weren't particular.

One of the latter was Gladys Jasmine, who threw her arms to the sky and died with a scream tearing from her lungs.

Fargo ran on to the stable.

Ransom Trayburn was saddling his chestnut. A pair of gun hands was doing likewise with other horses.

Kiley Strake stood between them and the wide doors, his feet planted wide.

Leaning the Henry against a door, Fargo strode in past the dead man with the pitchfork jutting from his chest. "Going somewhere?"

One of the gun hands hollered, and he and the other one swooped their hands for their hardware.

"No!" Kiley Strake shouted. "He's mine."

The pair froze, unsure what to do. They glanced at their boss.

Ransom Trayburn was in the act of tightening his cinch. Stepping back, he smiled smugly at Fargo. "Mister, you have grit. I'll give you that. But you just made your last mistake. Kiley, he's all yours."

Strake's thumb was hooked in his belt only a few inches from his pearl-handled Remington. "My prayers have been answered."

Fargo stopped when barely ten feet separated them. "You've been praying to die?"

Strake grinned. "You have more bark on you than most ten hombres I know."

Fargo waited. The other two had taken their hands off their six-guns and Trayburn was just standing there.

"That was some trick you pulled, getting out of the canyon," Strake said. "I never heard Mr. Trayburn cuss so much."

"Quit jabbering and get it over with," Ransom Trayburn snapped.

Strake nodded. "I reckon we should."

"Ladies first," Fargo said.

A gleam came into Strake's eyes and his body seemed to harden.

Fargo focused on Strake and only Strake. When the moment came it would be in a flash of movement.

"What are you waiting for?" Trayburn demanded.

"Don't rush me," Kiley Strake said.

Even though he was tensed and primed, the lightning suddenness of Strake's draw almost caught Fargo off guard. One instant his own hand was empty, the next he filled it with the Colt and the Colt and the Remington boomed simultaneously. Lead plucked at his sleeve as Kiley Strake lurched back a step. He fired again and Strake's left eye blew apart.

Like the wax on an overheated candle, Kiley Strake melted into a pile of bent limbs and spreading scarlet.

"Son of a bitch," Trayburn said.

The other two galvanized to life, their fingers splaying wide for the butts of their revolvers.

Fargo fanned the Colt twice.

Outside the stable, rifles were blasting and the Apaches were whooping and people were shrieking and fleeing into the night.

Inside, there were only the choked gasps of one of the dying shooters.

"Well, now," Ransom Trayburn said.

"Toss your hardware," Fargo commanded. "Two fingers only."

"What for? So you can shoot me down unarmed? Is that what you call fair?"

Fargo cocked the Colt. "I won't tell you twice."

"Fine," Trayburn said curtly. He very carefully threw his revolver at a pile of hay and it sank out of sight. "Do your worst. I won't beg for my life."

"Who asked you to?" Fargo shoved the Colt into his holster and bunched his fists. "Whenever you're ready."

Trayburn didn't hide his amazement. "Are you loco? You aim to beat me with your fists?"

"What was that about jabbering?" Fargo said.

Ransom Trayburn balled his hands and slowly advanced. "I was wrong before. *This* is your last mistake. I guess no one ever told you. I beat a man to death with my bare fists once."

"Was someone holding his arms for you?"

"That was your last insult."

Fargo had no more to say. He waded in and Trayburn threw a right. Blocking it, he drove a jab that caught Trayburn on the jaw and rocked him.

Stepping back, Trayburn shook his head to clear it. "Not bad," he said, smiling confidently. "But not good enough." And he came at Fargo swinging.

Fargo stood firm, trading blow for blow. Most he countered or slipped. Some got through. His cheek flared with pain, his ribs absorbed a solid left, his ear was clipped.

Trayburn smiled the whole while, he was that sure of himself.

They slugged hard and fierce, neither gaining an advantage. Then Trayburn showed his true nature by kicking at Fargo's knee. A quick grab, and Fargo had hold of Trayburn's ankle. He wrenched, upending him.

Ransom Trayburn got up slowly. His smile was gone. "All this over a damn horse." He gazed out at his house. "And look yonder. There's no stopping it. I'll have to rebuild, after."

"For you there won't be any after."

Fargo closed, and they went at it again. He didn't hold back. Their grunts and thuds mingled, and then he unleashed an uppercut that started down around his knees. It felt as if he broke every knuckle in his hand but it was worth it.

Flat on the ground, blood trickling from his mouth, Ransom Trayburn said, "Truce."

Not sure he'd heard correctly, Fargo responded with, "What?"

"A truce, damn you. You've wiped out most of my men. My house is burning. That's enough. How about if I admit I was wrong and pay you to make amends and we go our separate ways?"

"And you called me dumb as a stump?"

"How much do you want?"

"How much are you offering?"

Trayburn thought he was serious. Grinning slyly, he said, "Fifty thousand dollars. What do you say?"

"Stand up and we'll shake on it."

"I knew you'd see reason."

Fargo let him rise and punched him in the face.

Ransom Trayburn went berserk. He became a tornado, punching wildly. But his rage lasted for all of thirty seconds.

That was when Fargo slammed a right to the ribs and heard a sharp *crack*. He slammed a left to the other side and Trayburn gasped and tilted.

"Stop!"

Fargo smashed Trayburn's nose, rammed a left to his mouth, closed the swollen eye with a right cross. He side-stepped an overhand and delivered a blow to the kidney that caused Trayburn to cry out. He followed it with an uppercut to Trayburn's jaw. Teeth crunched and crimson sprayed and then Ransom Trayburn was on his knees.

"Please," he said, his mouth spewing blood. "I beg you."

Fargo took a step back. He slowly drew his Colt and slowly cocked it and slowly placed the muzzle close to Trayburn's forehead. "You steal my horse," he said, "I kill your ass."

The blast was loud.

Reloading, Fargo listened to the yips of the Apaches and the death rattle of a guest. He turned to go and then turned back and went through Trayburn's pockets. The roll of bills he found was thick enough to choke a goat.

Fargo was grinning when he swung on the Ovaro. He reined to the west and thought of Denver with its painted ladies and some of the best whiskey anywhere and poker games that never ended. "And a stall for you, big fella, with oats and a rubdown every day."

As if he understood, the stallion broke into a trot.

LOOKING FORWARD!
The following is the opening section of the next novel in the exciting Trailsman series from Signet:

TRAILSMAN #383
HIGH PLAINS MASSACRE

1861, the Black Hills—where the rumor of gold results in a river of blood.

Skye Fargo wasn't expecting anyone to try to kill him.

Fargo had sat in on a poker game at Paddy's, a tent saloon within shouting distance of Fort Laramie. The Irishman who ran it believed that one day soon a town would spring up and he would build a real saloon and make money hand over fist.

Fargo liked Paddy Welch. Paddy was one of the few men breathing who could down as much liquor as he could and not keel over from whiskey poisoning.

Fargo had just been dealt two queens and two tens and asked for a card and been given another queen. Lady Luck was riding on his shoulder. Now all he had to do was play it smart and build up the pot.

Then two things happened.

The first was a hand that tapped Fargo on the shoulder as someone cleared their throat. "Excuse me. Are you Skye Fargo, the scout?"

About to refill his glass, Fargo turned his head.

A young lieutenant in a clean uniform stood ramrod straight as if on parade, awaiting his answer.

"No," Fargo said.

"You answer the description I was given by Colonel Jennings. He said to look for a big man in buckskins, with a beard and blue eyes."

"Jennings, you say? Never met the man." Fargo filled his glass and set the bottle down.

"How peculiar." The lieutenant shifted his weight from one polished boot to the other and gnawed on his bottom lip. He had no chin to speak of and a pale complexion, and for a soldier, looked about as intimidating as a kitten. "Do you know this Fargo, then? Could you point him out to me?"

"Never met the man."

The other players were staring. One, in particular, had his mouth wide in surprise. As well he should, since Bear River Tom had been a friend of Fargo's for years. "Well, tits," he said, and laughed.

The lieutenant blinked. "Did you just call me tits, mister?"

"He calls everything tits," Fargo said. "They're all he ever thinks about. If he could, he'd eat them for breakfast."

"Would I ever," Bear River Tom agreed, with a vigorous bob of his chin. "Smeared with honey. Or maybe peaches and cream."

The lieutenant wasn't amused. "I don't know how tits got into this. I'm here on official business. And who might you be, anyhow? You wear buckskins. You're not Fargo, are you?"

"Do I have blue eyes?" Bear River Tom said, and opened his brown eyes as wide as they would open. "Am I so handsome that ladies rip their clothes off and throw themselves at my feet?"

"No," the lieutenant said. "Don't take this personal, but you're sort of ugly."

Fargo had just tilted his glass to his lips and burst out laughing and coughing.

"Tits and cream," Bear River Tom said, and introduced

himself. "Who are you, green boy? And why are you inter-rupting our game?"

The youngster gave a slight bow. "Lieutenant Archibald Wright, at your service. I'm not that green, I'll have you know. I've been on the frontier two months now."

"Two whole months," Bear River Tom said.

"Colonel Jennings would very much like to talk to this Fargo character," Lieutenant Wright said, "and he tasked me with finding him."

"Don't you hate being tasked?" Bear River Tom said.

"Have you any idea where I can find him?"

"He was planning to light a shuck for Denver," Fargo said.

Wright cocked his head. "I thought you just said you've never met the man."

"I heard it from the barkeep."

"Oh. Colonel Jennings will be terribly disappointed. The matter is most urgent."

Fargo's curiosity was piqued and he asked, "What is it about, anyhow?"

"You won't believe me if I told you," Lieutenant Wright said. "It sounds preposterous."

"Tell me anyway."

"I'm afraid the information is confidential."

"You can trust us, boy," Bear River Tom said. "I can keep my mouth shut except around tits."

"Must you mention them with every breath?" Lieutenant Wright shook his head. "I'd better keep searching in case this Fargo hasn't left yet. The colonel was most insistent." He gave another sort of bow and marched stiffly off.

"What that boy needs," Bear River Tom said, "is a night with a handful of tits. It'd take a lot of that starch out of him."

"Can we go five minutes without hearing about tits?" Fargo said.

Bear River Tom grinned and opened his mouth to say something. Suddenly his eyes grew wide again.

Fargo glanced over his shoulder, thinking that the young lieutenant was coming back. Instead, a much smaller man was coming at him with a knife poised to thrust.

National bestselling author

RALPH COMPTON

"A writer in the tradition of Louis L'Amour and Zane Grey!" —*Huntsville Times*

Available wherever books are sold or at
penguin.com

S543

THE LAST OUTLAWS
The Lives and Legends of Butch Cassidy and the Sundance Kid

by Thom Hatch

Butch Cassidy and the Sundance Kid are two of the most celebrated figures of American lore. As leaders of the Wild Bunch, also known as the Hole-in-the-Wall Gang, they planned and executed the most daring bank and train robberies of the day, with an uprecedented professionalism.

The Last Outlaws brilliantly brings to life these thrilling, larger-than-life personalities like never before, placing the legend of Butch and Sundance in the context of a changing—and shrinking—American West, as the rise of 20th century technology brought an end to a remarkable era. Drawing on a wealth of fresh research, Thom Hatch pushes aside the myth and offers up a compelling, fresh look at these icons of the Wild West.

Available wherever books are sold or at penguin.com

S0464